DEDICATED TO THOSE
WHO WILL NEVER LEAVE
MY SIDE

RULERS OF ASGARD THE MORTAL REALM

BY: CALEB BARNEY

CHAPTER ONE: THE CURSED GODDESS

EIGHT MONTHS PRIOR

Taliah stood in her bathroom staring into the mirror, admiring the right side of her face. It was so plush, so beautiful and full of life. It really was her best feature. She loved the shining silver color of her eye and her golden brown hair was long and curly. Taliah smiled at herself in the mirror, relishing every moment she could look at this part of her. It was the only thing about herself that she loved.

Her smile turned into a grimace as she turned her head to see the other half of her face. It felt like an eternity because she dreaded what she knew what she was about to lay eyes on. As her other half came into view, Taliah felt as if she was looking at a different person entirely.

The left side of her face looked dead. Her skin was as grey as a thundercloud, and the bone structure underneath was so prominent, it looked like it was just her skull. Her left eye had no color at all and was instead pearly white. Her hair was a mixture of brown and grey.

When she went to school, she was known as the "Half-dead girl" or teased for looking like a Halloween costume. Many of them actually did believe it was an amazing makeup job. However, Taliah knew that it was not so. Every day, she had to wake up and look in the mirror and she felt sick looking at the image that stared back.

She opened up the small drawer beside the sink and pulled out her foundation, custom made to match the color of the right side of her face.

She started to heavily apply the foundation, covering up the grey color of her left side. She didn't care for eyeliner, blush, or lipstick. All she wanted to do was make both sides match. She stood there gazing into the mirror for nearly an hour until she felt satisfied enough with the symmetry of her face. Once she was finished, she put back the foundation and grabbed a case of colored contacts.

She took out a silver contact lense and put it in her left eye. It didn't match her other eye perfectly, but it was the best she could do. Taliah looked at herself in the mirror again, imagining a life where she didn't have to worry about this, a life in which she was completely beautiful.

"Taliah! What the hell is taking you so long!" Taliah's step-dad, Noah Horde, was screaming from downstairs.

Taliah scrambled to put everything back, she had really lost track of time. She was becoming way too consistent at being tardy for school. Taliah didn't really care about it, but her dad really did, a bit too much. After the bathroom was presentable once again, Taliah put on her hoodie and backpack and rushed downstairs.

Knowing she already angered her dad made Taliah want to avoid him as much as possible. She sped walked towards the door, moving as swiftly and as quietly as possible, but it availed to nothing.

Noah reached his hand towards Taliah and firmly gripped her hood. Taliah almost fell backward when he pulled her back towards him.

"You know you can only be late for school so many times, girl." Taliah remained silent, saying anything while he was like this was a sure-fire way to get slapped across the face. Noah looked down on her in anger and hatred. He grabbed her by the chin and turned her head to see the dead side.

"It's your fault she's gone, all of this is your fault." Taliah was close to tears, wanting so badly just to run away, but running away never solved any of her problems. She was always found anyway. Noah turned her head again so he could see the pretty, life filled side. He took his hand away from her chin and caressed her plush cheek. "Such a

waste…get out of my sight."

She wouldn't wait for him to tell her a

second time. She busted through the front door, and

ran across the street, wiping tears away from her

eyes. Her contact started to fall out of place.

Taliah hated her life. Every moment ever

since she was born, her efforts to be happy were

met with a reminder that she couldn't. Ever since

she could go to school, she couldn't leave the house

without tears falling from her eyes. The only thing

that brought happiness in her life was her mother

Theresa, but she was gone. Ever since then, her

already miserable life became worse, so much

worse. So the tears falling from her eyes as she

walked to school that morning was nothing new.

Taliah reached her hands towards her face to wipe the tears again and realized that her foundation was probably washing away. The only thing that would make the day worse was being called "zombie-girl" for eight hours. She took out her phone to see the damage and decide whether or not she should skip school. She flipped the phone's camera around and was terrified by what she saw.

Her contact had fallen out, and her makeup slid off as if it was oil. Both of her eyes were pitch black and the deformed part of her face was covered with moving tattoos. She turned off the phone, praying it was just a camera filter. Then she noticed the smoke.

A black aura was coming out of her skin, enveloping her entire being in darkness. Before she could pass out from terror or run back home, her body was snatched from the world she was in and she was summoned to a realm outside of time.

When the dark cloud surrounding her faded away and she opened her eyes, Taliah found herself floating in mid-air in front of a larger-than-life tree. In front of the tree stood three young ladies who all looked identical with each other. They all wore the same gray robes and had the same silver hair. What Taliah found most unsettling was that they were all looking at her.

"Welcome to the realm between realms goddess of death," the one in the middle said. All Taliah could think was that she had finally lost her mind.

"What the hell is this," she asked frantically, more towards herself than the three ladies. The one on the right stepped forward and took a closer look at Taliah, who was still convinced that this couldn't be real.

"My my, she's going to say no." No? No to what? Taliah looked away from the ladies and pinched herself as hard as she could, thinking that this all had to be a dream. The pain from her arm told her the contrary. She began to think that the only way out of this dream was to play along.

"Who are you, what is this?"

"We are the Norns, the weavers of fate. You are here because it is time for you to wake up to your true nature."

Taliah furrowed her brow, "My true nature, what do you mean my true nature?"

The lady on her left rose her hand and the entirety of the space she was in was enveloped in fog. The tree had disappeared and it was replaced by the throne that sat upon a large black rock. Sitting on the throne was a dark figure that was shrouded in a thick dark mist. Its eyes were so black, they pierced through the darkness and seemed as if they had a light of their own.

The sister with her hand in the air spoke. "Many eons ago in the time before, you were the guardian of the underworld, Hel."

Taliah was speechless for many reasons. For one she was in the most frightening place she had ever seen. It was dark and scary and covered in mist that came from the figure on the throne. However, what stole Taliah's breath the most was the fact that if this was real, that scary figure sitting on that throne was probably her.

"Hel? Do you mean like Norse mythology? Are you saying…"

"Yes, you are the goddess of death." What. The. Hell. If this was a dream, it was starting to feel a little bit too real. She didn't even know that much about Norse mythology! She only knew snippets of it from movies and books. If this wasn't a dream, everything that Taliah knew had changed.

The Norns spoke again, "You have been summoned here because we have deemed it necessary that you reclaim your position in the realm of the dead, Helheim."

"To do what, sit on a chair?"

"No, to ensure that the spirits within never return to the realm of the living." None of this seemed like it could actually be happening. Not even a few minutes ago, Taliah was on her way to school. Now she was being told that she was a goddess and the goddess of death at that! How was any of this possible? Taliah thought about pinching herself again.

The Norn in the middle spoke up, "We know this is perplexing and sudden, but this is real, and we need a decision now."

Taliah thought about it for a second. She used to think that she would give anything to live a different life but switching it to watch dead people didn't sound that much better. "Would I be able to leave, like go anywhere else," she asked.

"No, Helheim and Niflheim will be your permanent abode." The sisters said in unison.

That was it, the deciding factor. While Taliah hated her life, at least she was able to change it one day. If this wasn't a dream and she said yes, Taliah would be stuck in this dank, musty and dark place. Here, she wouldn't have a choice. "Then no, I'm not gonna be stuck here forever."

"Think wisely Hel," The Norns said, "Though you may avoid this for a time, you can't avoid who you are."

"Then I'll wait for fate to decide. Please let me go back home."

The Norns grunted in irritation, and lifted their hands, "You will return to Midgard, but with your godly abilities. We will meet again soon."

Suddenly, a blinding bright light that shone in all colors surrounded Taliah. She closed her eyes and threw her hand to her face. When she opened her eyes she was back on the ground, standing on the sidewalk. Everything looked the same, but something inside her felt... different.

CHAPTER TWO: A DATE IN

THE GARDEN

PRESENT DAY

"So just like that," Jacob exclaimed, "We
are letting them throw a birthday party for you."

Javi chuckled, "Not all of them, just Aegir.
he did it in the old era anyway." Jacob grunted.
Even though he himself was a frost giant, he didn't
like inviting any of his kind to Asgard, and now
Javi had hired one to throw a party. If they were still
crooked, it would be an excellent opportunity to
spike Javi's drink or something.

"I'm just saying man, it has only been six months since we stopped fighting them. Are you sure we can trust them?"

Javi scoffed, Jacob wasn't really screaming trustworthy himself. Javi lifted his tunic and exposed the stab wound in his side. "I still chose to trust you, didn't I?"

"Come on man," Jacob groaned, "How long are you going to hold that against me, I told you I had a plan."

"Your plan sucked," Javi chuckled. It was funny now, but the first couple of months after the battle, Javi gave Jacob the silent treatment. "Either way, having this party is a good way of solidifying our peace agreement."

"Well if they do end up killing you, I call dibs on the spear." Javi chuckled again. Little did Jacob know, Tyr beat him to the punch.

After a little more friendly banter, Jacob left to go to Svartalfheim. He had decided to learn dark elfin magic from the Dokkalfar, the dark elves. Javi went back to the palace to meet up with Fiora. He had promised her a ride across Asgard since neither of them had really traveled across the realm since they got there. Javi was looking forward to it, but first, he had to figure out where Fiora was hiding.

He knew that she wouldn't be in the throne room, they only ever went there when there was something important to talk about. The only other place she could be was in his room. Javi ran up the stairs and down the hall. He stopped in front of the wooden door that led to his abode and slowly

opened it, just in case Fiora jumped out at him.

"Fiora? Are you in here?" Javi said as he

walked in the room ever so cautiously. When he

opened the door fully, who he saw definitely wasn't

Fiora.

"What's up man," said Tyr who was sitting

on Javi's bed. Javi walked into the forest of his

room and made his way towards the back.

"Tyr, what are you doing in my room?"

Tyr chuckled, "I know it's a little bit weird,

but Fiora asked me to wait for you here."

"Why?"

"She wanted me to tell you to meet her

under the tree." Under the tree. The moment he said

it, Javi knew what he was talking about. Not too far

away from the palace, there was a small grove. In

the middle of it was an incredibly large tree. Javi

figured that the tree was supposed to be a

representation of the world tree Yggdrasil, the

universal tree that contained the nine realms.

Fiora and Javi sat underneath that tree in the

grove almost every single day. It was peaceful and

serene, and if you were there at the right time, you

could see the sunset fall behind the palace as the

stars came out to take its place.

Javi left the palace and went to the stable to

grab his eight-legged horse. Fiora always treasured

a nice long walk, but Javi seldom traveled long

distances without Sleipnir. As soon as he walked

into the stable, the gallant white horse whinnied in

excitement.

"Good morning boy, how are you doing?"

Javi asked. The horse didn't speak English (or at all), but Javi felt that Sleipnir had been bored out of his mind. Javi jumped on his back and said, "Take me to the tree." With that, Sleipnir whinnied even more excitedly and ran out of the stable.

Ordinarily, a casual stroll to the tree would make a good two hours. However, Sleipnir was the fastest known horse throughout all of the nine realms. At a full gallop, it would take only a minute and a half. Javi held tightly to the reigns, careful not fall off as the horse ran at full speed. In seconds they were outside of castle grounds, the grove of trees already visible in the distance. Before a minute was up, they were already in the shade of the trees.

Sleipnir slowed to a trot, carefully weaving his large body through the maze of the grove. Finally, there she was, sitting underneath the sparkling tree. Javi couldn't believe how graceful she looked as the glowing green leaves fell and settled around her. Her red hair was a perfect contrast against the forest of green.

"Hello m'lady," Javi said, "How fare thee this fine morning?"

Fiora giggled, "Do you have to talk like Shakespeare every single time."

Javi smiled as he dismounted Sleipnir, "You know, we probably talked like that all the time in the old age."

Fiora stood up, "Get over here you weirdo." Javi didn't have to be told twice. He quickly closed the distance between them and took Fiora in his

arms. He looked into her one eye and remembered

the sacrifice she chose to make for the nine realms.

His heart skipped a beat as the vibrant green color

of her eye met his golden brown one. He brought

his face closer to hers to kiss her, but she backed

away. "Let's go for our ride first."

Javi was thrown off. Usually, when they

kissed, Fiora was the instigator. Nonetheless, Javi

honored her wishes and helped her onto Sleipnir.

He jumped on after she was comfortable.

Javi commanded Sleipnir to leave the grove

and travel towards the mountains east of the castle.

The ride there was mostly silent and Javi couldn't

put his finger on why it felt so awkward. He thought

that they had passed this phase already, that it was

all uphill since they kissed in the graveyard. He was convinced he was doing something wrong.

Before long they had reached the mountain and began to travel through the split that led to the beautiful garden that grew behind. When they reached it, Javi dismounted Sleipnir and helped Fiora down. Sleipnir laid down, understanding that Fiora wanted alone time with Javi.

Walking into the garden, Javi and Fiora were taken aback by its breathtaking beauty. Flowers of all colors sprouted from the ground, apple trees towered overhead. It seemed that the garden itself had a pinkish glow. At the center of the garden was one of the trees that provided the gods with Idunn Apples. Javi and Fiora settled underneath it.

"What's wrong Fiora?" Javi asked, incredibly concerned over her silence throughout the ride there.

Fiora took a deep breath and responded, "I've been thinking a lot, about all of this, about us."

Javi furrowed his brow, "About us? Why? Is something wrong?"

"No not really, it's just that now I see how everything we know now isn't made by us, it's made by fate." This answer only confused Javi even more. Sure the weavers of fate (or as Javi called them, the Norns) had a lot to do with their current position, but he didn't see how it connected to him and Fiora, and their relationship. Fiora could see Javi's confusion and elaborated.

"I just want to be sure that what we have with each other is our choice."

Javi took a sigh of relief. Considering what he had been contemplating to be the problem, this wasn't that bad.

"Fiora, I know the feelings I have for you, and I know that I make the choice to love you, just like I chose to trust Jacob after what he did." He put his hand on her face, "I choose to fall in love with you every single day, and that is never going to change, no matter who says what."

Fiora grabbed his hand and held it tight, "I love you Javi."

Javi smiled and pulled closer to Fiora and this time, she pulled closer too.

CHAPTER THREE: THE DARKEST GIFT

"Why," Taliah whispered to herself, "Why me?" She sat on the cold hard wooden floor of the dance studio. It was a few hours before her ballet practice, but she wanted to be by herself as much as possible, especially after her experience with the Norns.

She had been contemplating what they told her for eight months. She tried to convince herself it was a dream at first, but then she learned she had… abilities. First, it started slow. She would wake up and find black smoke leaking from her skin, pouring all over the ground. Eventually, she learned how to control it and could make smoke come out of her hands at will. However, she still didn't understand what that smoke could do, at least until it touched a bird.

She didn't mean to do anything to it, the bird just happened to land in front of her as she was practicing using her power. The smoke completely engulfed the bird and sunk into its small body. It immediately fell down and began convulsing, thrashing its body against the ground. Then it fell still, and it never moved again.

Now here she was sitting in that empty dance studio, fully aware that she was indeed the goddess of death, just as those three ladies said. She was scared of herself and what she could do, her mind was in chaos. All she wanted was a moment of peace, she wanted to dance in the dark.

She stood and walked to a speaker sitting on a table by a wall and pushed play. Beethoven's *Moonlight Sonata* began to fill the once still and silent room. Taliah instinctively began to perform as she had been taught all those times before.

With her eyes closed, she pranced about the studio, every move precise and fluid. This was her escape, her peace in the midst of a storm. She danced away the pain and all of the bad memories she carried. All of those evil things her peers told her, all of those sneer remarks. Every time she was struck by her father, every time she was told she was worthless. She danced it all away and began to feel free.

In the midst of her dancing, unbeknownst to her, Taliah's dark power began to fall from her skin and pour all over the floor of the dance studio. The lights began to flicker, and the air became bitterly cold. For the first time in her life, Taliah felt something that she had never felt before, power and control.

Taliah stopped dancing and opened her eyes. She saw the black smoke crawling all over the ground, but this time she wasn't disgusted by it. This was her, and extension of who she was. She was powerful, and that made her feel worthy. Instead of staying for practice, Taliah decided to go home. She grabbed her duffle bag and walked out of the dance studio, the black smoke followed her footsteps.

The walk to her house didn't take long, it was right around the corner. When she got to the front door, she could tell that her father was home and based on the bottles of beer on the ground, he had been drinking.

"I just have to get upstairs," Taliah whispered to herself. She opened the front door and walked through, carefully making her way towards the stairs. Slowly she crept and inched her way there, careful not to step on any of the creaky floorboards. When she got close enough, she launched herself onto the stairs and bolted towards her bedroom. She ran inside, locked the door, and breathed out a sigh of relief.

"What's the rush sweetheart?" Taliah's heart dropped to her stomach. She turned around and saw Noah sitting on her bed. She looked down and saw that he was holding a picture of his ex-wife, and a gun.

"You know Taliah," Noah said with slurred speech, "I've been thinking a lot about you, and what a curse you have been to me."

Taliah slowly raised her hands, not wanting to make any sudden moves. "Hey let's think about this okay," she said, hoping she could talk sense into him. "You're drunk, maybe you should just go lay down."

Noah scoffed and looked back down at the picture. "You know we were happy before, before you. We loved each other, laughed with each other." A tear began to fall from his eye, "Then we adopted you, and everything changed."

This rant wasn't something that Taliah wasn't already used to. Noah blamed her for everything ever since her mother left him. There was nothing Taliah could have done to change that, but Noah was convinced that his adoptive daughter had evil inside of her, no matter what anyone said.

"Taliah I just want to be happy again. I just want to live the rest of my life in peace, and the only way I can do that is if I get rid of you!"

Noah raised his gun and aimed it at Taliah, and before she could shout in protest, he fired. Taliah felt the bullet go through her stomach and out through her back. Her hands rushed to hold the wound, but when she touched where it should have been, the wound wasn't there. Then she realized something, she wasn't in pain, it didn't hurt at all.

Taliah turned and saw a bullet hole in the door right behind her. Her horror turned into relief, and then anger.

She turned back towards Noah and slowly started to walk towards him. Noah backed away terrified and shot at her two more times, still doing her no harm. The closer Taliah got to her Noah, the more she was consumed by rage. Every scar, every derogatory word, every time he had ever hurt her fueled her power. Her eyes turned so dark, they began to absorb the light surrounding her, darkening the room. Dark runes began to travel across the dead side of her face.

She stopped walking and bent down, Noah's back was against the wall. They were eye to eye. Noah raised his fist and swung it and Taliah's chin, his last attempt to escape, but it availed to nothing. His hand went straight through her face, causing her no harm.

She smiled, "You can't hurt me anymore, no one can." She raised her hand and touched the side of Noah's face, "How does it feel dad," she asked, "To be completely powerless to what happens around you?"

Still smiling, tears fell from her eyes, "I will not let you hurt me anymore. I'm finally going to be free." Black smoke leaked out of her hand and into Noah's head. The veins in his face turned black and he began to gasp for air, choking on his own breath.

"I *hate* you so much," Taliah growled through her teeth, "And you deserve much worse than this." Blood poured out of Noah's nose and his eyes turned pale white. His skin became grey as he continually fought for air. His cheekbones poked through his skin and life began to drain from his flesh. When Taliah moved her hand away, Noah fell to his side, dead as a doornail.

Taliah looked down upon his body, upon what she did. She knew there were consequences, but she was prepared to pay them, so long as he was no longer alive to torment her.

"You are no less powerful than you were in the Old Age," a voice with a heavy accent said from behind her. Taliah whipped around and saw an old bearded man standing in the doorpost, holding a long crooked brown cane. He wore a tattered brown tux and stared directly at Taliah.

"Who the hell are you?" Taliah demanded.

"I am Modi, the second son of Thor."

Taliah was tempted to doubt that answer, but after what she just did, something like this was very much possible. "What do you want from me," She asked with a slight shake in her voice.

"I am not here for what you can do for me, I'm here for what I can do for you."

"What are you talking about?"

Modi smiled and walked into the room, "Of all the gods, you have the darkest gift, so dark that even Odin feared you. That is why you were cast into Helheim."

Taliah recalled the conversation she had with the weavers of fate, "If you are going to ask me to go back to Helheim, don't. I already told those freaks at the tree I wouldn't go back."

Modi chuckled, "I am not asking you to rule over Helheim, I'm offering you the chance to rule over Asgard."

Even with the sparse knowledge that Taliah had of Norse mythology, she knew that Asgard was much different than Helheim, it was paradise.

"Taliah, you can be the queen of Asgard. There is only one loose end that you need to burn."

Taliah was listening and intrigued, but how was she supposed to answer that? She had just recently figured out she was a goddess, and now she was told that she could be the queen of a place that wasn't supposed to be real. She knew this was real, but it didn't feel like it.

Modi saw her mind racing for something to say, "You are more powerful than you know Taliah,

and your power can save the nine realms from
destruction."

Taliah furrowed her brow, "What do you
mean?"

"The gods that brought the end of the Old
Age upon us have risen from the dead. Odin, Thor,
Loki, they all have returned." Lightning flashed in
Modi's eyes, he hated speaking their names. "They
will bring the end upon us again if they are not dealt
with."

Taliah finally understood what he was
asking, "You want me to kill them?"

"Yes, and in doing so, save the nine realms."

"Even if I agreed to do this, how would I
even start? How would I get to them?"

Modi chuckled again, "Come with me and I will show you."

Taliah looked at Noah's body as it lay on her bed. If she refused, she would be on the run for the rest of her life on the run because of what she did. If she accepted, after doing this one terrible thing, she would be a queen, she would be free. At this point, she had nothing to lose. Her one colored eye returned to its natural silver color.

"Where are we going?"

CHAPTER FOUR:

AEGISHJÁLMUR

Two weeks have passed and it was finally the big day. As much as he was excited about the party, Javi wished that Aegir didn't have to kick him out of Asgard to set it up. However, it did present a good opportunity to tie up a loose end he had forgotten about. While he was in Svartalfheim (the realm of the dwarves and dark elves), Javi made a promise to the legendary Dwarf, Brokkr. He promised he would come back after the battle with Ymir. No better time to do it than the present.

Javi had walked through the portal in the realm travel room two hours ago and had finally come upon the mountain that the dwarves had embedded themselves in. It seemed like a distant memory now, but Javi could remember the fight he had with the stone dragon here, and much like the mountains that still bore the damage of that battle, Javi still bore the scars the dragon gave him.

He approached the entrance to the gargantuan mountain, which was blocked by a not-so-big magical stone. There was no way to open the gate with brute strength. The only way inside was to know the magic of the dwarves or be a trusted member of the Aesir, the tribe of gods that resided in Asgard.

The dwarves had infused the weapons with dwarven magic, creating a kind of key to get into the mountain. Javi took his golden spear, Gungnir, and touched the tip of the spear against the rock that safeguarded the entrance. The spear began to glow intensely and the light coming from it began to travel across the shaft like liquid towards the rock. As the light touched it, the rock faded away in a magnificent light.

Javi walked through the entrance, having to duck his head a little bit. As soon as he walked into the mountain, Javi was met with the intense odor of burning metal. It was musty and incredibly warm and if he was honest, Javi didn't really like it that much. However, the dwarves inside found it to be just to their liking. Inside the mountain, hundreds of dwarves hobbled around, carrying metals and tools to forge weapons for the gods.

"Well ain't it about damn time!" A yell came from behind a group of dwarves trying to pick up an iron boulder. The voice was garbled and raspy, but Javi knew it well. The famous dwarf, Brokkr, hobbled from behind the struggling dwarves and went straight to Javi. "I was beginnin' to think that you were dead again already." The long-bearded dwarf laughed and snorted, thinking he was the funniest dwarf in Svartalfheim.

"Sorry," Javi said with a chuckle, "I meant to come sooner but Ymir tore me up pretty good."

"Did yah kill him for it," Brokkr said earnestly.

"Uh well no, not really," Javi responded.

"NO, the hell you mean no!" Brokkr grumbled. He hobbled past Javi to make sure the sealing to the mountain fully reappeared. "You know, I don't really have anything against the bastard, but makin' peace treaties with Jotnar isn't really an "Odin" thing to do.

He was right, that wasn't an Odin thing to do. In the Old Age, Javi's past self completely dismembered Ymir. Javi walked up towards Brokkr and said, "I know it's not what you're used to, but I want to make sure we do things right this time."

Brokkr grunted, "Well I hope Ymir is kind enough not to flatten Asgard with his big toe."

Javi chuckled. Even when Brokkr was noticeably irritated, he still couldn't help but make jokes.

"So tiny Odin," Brokkr continued, "What did yah come all the way here for."

"Before I went to fight Ymir, I asked about your brother Eitri. You told me to come back after the battle."

Suddenly Brokkr's face darkened, "Yes, yes I did, didn't I." He looked towards all the dwarves hobbling around with equipment and materials, then back at Javi. "Alright then, follow me."

Brokkr led Javi through the maze of the mountain. Almost everywhere, dwarves were walking to and fro, fulfilling the duties each of them was assigned. However, the farther and farther they got from the entrance, the number of dwarves surrounding them diminished. Eventually, they happened upon the entrance to Brokkr's personal workshop.

"After Ragnarok, the Dokkalfar and the dwarves got into a bit of a disagreement. Before long that little beef turned into a bloody war." Brokkr hobbled over to a table with a bunch of forgery equipment strewn over it. "Most of the dwarves chose to fight against them, but not Eitri. Eitri was a peace lovin fella." Brokkr moved around the clutter on the table, looking for something.

Javi could hear he was slowly starting to cry. He wanted to give him a hug, but he figured Brokkr wasn't one for physical contact. "What happened to him," Javi inquired.

Brokkr turned and said, "I don't know. Soon after the scrapping started, he up and left Svartalfheim."

"Maybe he's just escaping the violence, I'm sure he'll be back."

Brokkr scoffed, "Do you know how old I am boy?" Javi stayed silent and Brokkr turned back to the table. "Truth is, I don't rightly know myself, but it has been millions of years since those bloody battles. If Eitri wanted to come back, he'd be here."

Brokkr wiped a tear from his eyes. "Promise me Javi, promise that if you find him on any of ye ventures, you kick his rear end and bring him home."

Javi chuckled a little bit, but he could tell Brokkr was serious. Ordinarily, Javi didn't like making promises because of the off chance that he wouldn't be able to keep it. Promises were dangerous but at that moment, it was the right

decision.

"I promise Brokkr. If I find him."

The dwarf smiled, "Well if that be the case,

I want to make sure you have all you need to do it."

Brokkr picked up something from the table and

brought it to Javi. It was a golden ring with a silver

symbol at the center.

Javi recalled seeing a symbol like this

before, but he didn't really know what it was.

"Wow, it's a really nice ring." He said while

grabbing it from the dwarf's hand.

"It be more than a ring. This here is a shield

and a magical one at that." A shield? There was

nothing shield-like about it. But as the man said, it

was magical. There was more to it than meets the

eye. Brokkr continued, "That be a protective stave

on it, Aegishjálmur."

Javi remembered. Aegishjálmur meant

"Helm of Awe". Legend said it could protect its

user from getting bruised up too badly.

"How do you make it work," Javi asked.

"Just hold it out in front of you, like any

other shield." Javi put the ring on his left middle

finger and held it out as if he was holding a shield

and immediately, a ticking sound emerged from the

ring. In a few seconds, a bright golden light

illuminated the cave. As it dimmed, Javi could see

that the ring had turned into a large round golden

shield with the runic stave at the center.

Brokkr laughed heartily in pride,

"Impressive ain't she!"

Javi smiled, it was indeed impressive. It felt

sturdy and unbreakable, but it was light and easy to

control. "You have outdone yourself with this one

man!"

The dwarf couldn't stop smiling, "That

shield will stop any harm coming your way, just

make sure it's in front of you."

Whenever it came to weapons, armor or otherwise, Javi knew he could trust Brokkr to always deliver. Javi relaxed his arm and the shield disappeared. "Thank you Brokkr, you're the best.

"Ah go on with yah," Brokkr chuckled, "It's my pleasure, but don't forget your promise." He wouldn't, Javi would make sure of it. He was about to ask if he could see any of the other stuff the dwarf may have created, but he remembered something he had nearly forgotten about.

Aegir and his two assistants were probably finished setting up Javi's birthday party. If he didn't hurry back to Asgard, he would be late to his own birthday party.

"I'll look for Eitri, Brokkr," Javi said. "But right now I have to head back home. I'm late for a party."

Brokkr grunted and said, "Very well, but before you go, let me give you some food for thought." Brokkr walked up to Javi, "Your friend Jacob, I know he's gallivanting with the Dokkalfar. You might want to be careful with that."

"How come," Javi asked.

"The magic of the Dark Elves has a tendency to corrupt the user. It's the catch that comes with power." Javi appreciated the warning, but it wasn't anything Javi was surprised by. He had Jacob train in mental fortitude before he left. Javi tried to reassure Brokkr of this, but the dwarf just shook his head and said, "Alright then, but don't be surprised if he comes back a bit more sinister than when he left."

Javi understood, even though he was sure Brokkr was wrong. Jacob wasn't the one to be tricked, he was the trickster. If the Dark Elves tried anything funny, Javi had no doubt that Jacob would be five steps ahead of them. He left the mountain of the dwarves and made his way to the realm travel room. It was time to celebrate his birthday.

CHAPTER FIVE:

SOMETHING HAPPENED

"I'm sorry," Taliah exclaimed, "You want me to what?" Modi had brought her to the clouds, using his power to keep them suspended in the air. The pale moonlight dimly illuminated their faces.

Modi was annoyed at the girl, even though he expected this part of the deal to cause disagreement. "In order to bring the gods to Midgard, we must cover the realm in a darkness that would beg their attention."

"And how do you expect me to do that?"

Sparks of electricity ran through Modi's blue eyes. He took a deep breath and turned his eyes to the ground. Below them were moving cars and flashing lights, machines that Modi had watched mortals create. For thousands of years, he had seen them be born into this mortal world, grow old and die. It was a constant cycle that Modi had grown accustomed to.

"Tell me, dear, are there good people in this world?"

Taliah looked at Modi confused. That wasn't an answer to her question, but it was a question she felt compelled to answer. "Um… well, I haven't met any, but I'm sure there are some good people."

Modi chuckled, "Allow me to offer a word of wisdom. There is no such thing as good or bad, just beings that decide according to their own intentions."

Taliah remained silent, what was she supposed to say. It seemed that the old man was ranting to her. Modi turned to her and said, "Over the course of history, mortals lived to die for a cause that they believe will one day change their small world. They die in the name of love and hatred, freedom and bondage. If only they realized they truly died for nothing."

At this point, Taliah was so confused, she had to make sure that Modi knew he was making no sense to her. "What are you telling me this for man?"

"So that you understand why I must ask you to cast a plague on this world."

"WHAT!?" A plague? He wanted her to make the whole world sick, maybe even killing a lot of people. "Modi I agreed to kill the gods you warned me about, not the whole damn planet!"

"Why does it trouble you? These beings care not about your life, why is it that theirs is so important?"

He was right, not one person that Taliah had ever met cared about her. Still, that wasn't a justifiable reason for genocide. "Dude there are kids on this planet, babies that won't get a chance to decide who they are going to be!"

"And if they die, more will be born to take their place." Taliah was speechless, so Modi continued, "Do not let a false sense of compassion blind you Hel, this present time means nothing in the eyes of eternity."

"Modi this is evil."

"No, it is necessary for the salvation of the nine realms. You will see, one-thousand years for them will be a fleeting moment for us. The world will repopulate and rebuild, as it always does, but this time it will thrive because no Aesir will be alive to taint the universe any longer."

A tear fell from Taliah's eye, not because she was sad, but because she knew he was right. She knew that she would have to do what he was asking. Modi could see that he nearly had her convinced, all he had to do was put the nail in the coffin.

"Hel, their sacrifice today will be the preservation of eternity."

The nail had been struck, and Taliah was fully convinced. With tears filling her eyes, she stretched out her hands towards the earth below. She thought of what she had done to her father, what she felt when that power burst from inside of her. She remembered the feeling of hatred and anger, bitterness and resentment.

Suddenly, an enormous plume of black smoke emerged from her hands and descended upon the earth. Inside of it, sickness and pestilence churned, ready to inflict whoever it touched with the worst disease ever. One that would cause pain and suffering that would last for years. One that could be the end of the world if it remained for too long. Taliah didn't want to do it, but it was necessary. She had to do whatever it took to save the realms, even if it meant she had to be a monster.

Javi had expected something complex for his birthday set-up in Asgard, but he wasn't expecting something like this. It seemed like somehow, Aegir had changed Asgard around entirely. The sky was dark, but the realm was still bright. Little specks of light were floating around in the air, like miniature stars.

Javi walked out of the realm travel room, into the throne room. Once inside, Javi saw a trail of colorful light leading out of the castle, past the fjord, and out of the castle grounds. Javi had a feeling that he was supposed to follow it.

As soon as Javi walked out of the castle grounds, he realized one glaring difference in the appearance of the realm. The once flat and open fields leading up to the castle was now a large and endless forest.

Javi was blown away! How was it at all possible to create an entire forest in a few hours! Aegir and his friends really did go all out with this. Wide-eyed, Javi continued to follow the bright stream of light as it twisted and wound throughout the maze of the forest.

As he walked deeper and deeper into the peace of the trees, Javi noticed a few things that were going on simultaneously. For one, every time he took a step, the grass beneath him glowed in a magnificent white light. Javi was mesmerized by it, wondering how Aegir could have possibly accomplished this. The second thing he noticed was the constant boom of a drum.

Javi recognized the slow hypnotic beat, "Boom boom...boom boom...boom boom." It was the beat of a Viking war drum. Javi knew there wasn't going to be a battle at the end of the trail of light, but the beat of the drum pounded inside of his heart. Somehow, the mere sound of it started to spark something in Javi that he hadn't felt in the months since the battle in Jotunheim. His skin started getting warm and tingly, his one eye began to glow brightly in glorious golden light. The drums began to spark within him, the spirit of battle.

As soon as his eye began to glow, Javi walked into a clearing in the forest, a clearing that was filled to the brim with those that resided in

Asgard. Aegir stood in front of all of them, he would be the first to greet Javi. Even though he was a frost giant, Aegir more closely resembled an Asgardian. His skin was pale but he had a long brown braided beard. His hair was braided all the way down his back. At his sides were his two assistants, Fimafeng and Eldir.

Aegir stepped forward and spoke, "Itreker, Runatyr, Hjaldrgegnir, Hooded One." Javi had nearly forgotten how many nicknames he had. "In the Old Age, Odin was known as the enemy of my kind. The end of his spear brought judgment down upon us. However, we do not live in the Old Age anymore, and we do not live under the rule of the same Odin." Applause erupted from the crowd standing behind Aegir.

Aegir was proud of himself, it was the first party he had organized for the gods since the Old Age. The fact that he still had the gift made his spirit warm. "Today," he continued, "We celebrate the one who will lead the nine realms into an age of glory. I present to you the king of Asgard, Odin, our Allfather!"

Everyone began to cheer and clap. All this love made a tear fall from Javi's glowing eye. A few of the Valkyrie that knew how to play music brought some of the old instruments up from the storeroom. They began to fill the air with the sound of old Nordic music, as per Aegir's request. At first, no one knew how to dance to it, but someone started acting like they were jumping around a fire and everyone kind of just followed in their footsteps.

Javi walked up to Aegir, still astonished that his hands created all of this. "How in the world did you manage to do this all in a few hours."

A deep proud chuckle emerged from the jotunn's throat, "A little bit of work, a little bit of magic."

Suddenly, someone came up behind Javi and grabbed his hand, "And a little bit of insight," it was Fiora. She had helped Aegir figure out what Javi would most appreciate. She was the one that recommended the forest as the setting for the party. Javi turned to Fiora and smiled. He kissed her on the forehead and thanked Aegir one more time before going to look for everyone else.

The rest of the court of Asgard was pretty

well hidden within the mass of the Valkyrie and

Light Elves. That was the one flaw Javi could find

in Aegir's set up, too many people were invited.

Eventually, he happened upon Damien, who was

trying to impress some of the Valkyrie with his

magical hammer, Mjolnir. He was shooting a

stream of lightning at a nearby tree when he caught

sight of Javi.

"Well here he is, the birthday boy," he

shouted as he hooked Mjolnir back on his waist.

Damien walked up to Javi and gave him an

unnecessarily tight bear hug. It didn't help that the

red-head chose to wear his iron armor for the

occasion. Damien picked up on the fact that his hug

may have indeed been a bit too much and let Javi go.

"Thanks, Damien, it's good to see you," he said as cordially as possible, "Haven't seen you around in a good few weeks, where have you been?"

"Went to go sightseeing in some of the other realms, was pretty cool until I got to Muspelhiem."

Javi's eyes widened, "You went to Muspelhiem!?" Muspelhiem was the realm of fire, and supposedly uninhabitable unless you happened to be the fire jotunn Surtr.

Damien smiled pridefully, "Yup, it wasn't all that fun, but I get bragging rights for it!" Suddenly a wasp flew in front of Damien's face and flew in circles around his head. If there was one thing that Damien couldn't stand, it was stinging insects. He swung his hands at the wasp frantically, he was about five seconds from running away as fast as he could.

The wasp, on the other hand, was very calm and collected. It dodged every single one of Damien's swings and went in for its own attack. The wasp stung Damien's wrist and flew behind Javi. As Damien howled in pain, the wasp's body began to glow, and in a bright purple flash, the wasp turned into someone who Javi and Damien knew very well. Jacob had apparently returned from Svartalfheim, sooner than he said he would. He doubled over laughing, mainly at how scared Damien was when he was flying around his face.

Damien was livid, "You little twerp!" He rushed to Jacob who was still overcome with laughter and grabbed him by his neck.

Javi, seeing where this was going, jumped towards Damien and grabbed his arm. "Hey! Let's not kill each other on my birthday!" Damien grunted and released his grip and walked away. Just then Tyr walked up to Javi with a concerned look on his face.

"What happened," he asked, "Is everything okay?"

"Yeah," Javi responded, "Jacob just pulled another prank on him." Tyr's look of concern faded away and he started to chuckle.

"Damien's gonna kill Jacob if he's not careful. I'm going to try and calm him down before he starts knocking down trees." Tyr ran to where Damien stormed off to, hoping he didn't already put a crater in the ground.

"I'm telling you, man," Jacob said after he caught his breath, "That dude really can't take a joke."

Javi turned to Jacob and shook his head, "Stinging him might have been a step too far."

Jacob scoffed, "C'mon man, the dude got engulfed by the flames of a dragon before. A little wasp sting is nothing to him."

Before Javi could respond, a bright light that shone in all colors illuminated the entirety of the realm. That could only mean that someone had just used the Bifrost and was now in Asgard. However, no one should have come at all. Every realm was informed that Javi's birthday was being celebrated.

No creature from any realm had permission to

interrupt unless it was a true emergency, and Javi

had a feeling deep in his gut that it was indeed an

emergency.

Javi told Aegir to keep the party going while

he and the rest of the court of Asgard went to

investigate. Honoring his wish, Aegir continued to

entertain the Valkyrie and Elves. Javi gathered,

Fiora, Tyr, Jacob, and Damien, and headed for the

castle. When they entered the throne room, their

hearts sank as their eyes met that of the god of the

sea, Njord. Beside him stood Daniel and Ryan. Javi

had not seen any of them since the battle in

Jotunheim. Daniel walked up to Javi, his pure white

eyes looked as if he had seen every ghost in existence.

"Javi," he began, "Something... something happened."

"What happened?" Javi asked, his voice shaking a little bit.

"Midgard, I can't see it anymore."

CHAPTER SIX: THE GAME HAS BEGUN

Javi sat down on his throne and felt like the weight of the world rested upon his shoulders. Once he believed that the throne was a symbol of power and authority. It was supposed to make the one who sat in it feel like there was nothing that could stand against them. Javi now felt that the throne only told him that something was very wrong.

Javi had Njord, Daniel, and Ryan stand before him in the throne room to further explain the reason for their arrival. Daniel and Ryan chose not to assume what once was their thrones since they chose to live in Vanaheim instead of Asgard (mainly because Jacob was still there). Daniel stepped forward nervously and spoke first.

"A few hours ago, I felt a disturbance on Midgard. It was more of a feeling than an actual thing."

Javi rubbed his eyes, "Daniel, you said you couldn't see Midgard at all. I want to know why."

"I don't have an answer for that Javi! After I felt that disturbance I tried looking at the realm, but it was covered in darkness." Javi didn't really know what that could mean. Maybe there just happened to be something wrong with Daniel's sight. However, Javi knew that Daniel wouldn't be there if it was just something wrong with him. Javi remained silent, trying to think of a possible reason as to why the realm was hidden from Daniel's eyes.

Njord picked up on Javi's pondering and said, "I have only seen this happen once before. In the old age, before Odin cast Hel into Niflheim, she was welcome in the court of Asgard." That was pretty different from the tales that Javi had read before. He thought that Odin threw her in Niflheim immediately upon seeing her.

Njord continued, "As she grew older, her powers became more potent, but at the time she had no idea how to control them. Before long the entirety of the realm was covered in her darkness and almost every god that resided within fell ill." Njord shivered as if he could remember it like it happened yesterday. "Against Loki's wishes, your past self cast Hel out of Asgard and charged her to rule over the land of the dead."

At first, Javi was confused as to why Njord was telling him a story when he wanted answers, but then he started to put two and two together. Asgard was once covered in darkness when Hel was present, which meant that Hel had to be present in Midgard. As Damien once said, not all of the reincarnated gods assumed the role their past selves had.

Now more or less understanding the problem, Javi began to think of a solution. He could only think of one. "If Hel really is killing everyone in Midgard, we have to go down there and stop her."

Njord laughed mockingly, "Noble, but foolish. At full power, Hel is stronger than all of you combined. She wields the power of death, and not even you could beat that in the end."

Javi looked at Njord disgusted. What else were they supposed to do, wait until Hel snuffed the life out of every creature on earth? "Njord, we aren't just going to sit here and do nothing knowing we can do something."

"Let's examine the facts Javi. If we go down there, finding her is going to take time, and the longer we are down there, the more we are exposed to the pestilence she has soaked into Midgard."

"Njord, it is our responsibility. We would do the same thing for you." At first, Njord looked shocked, as if he didn't think Javi was capable of such noble behavior. Then his look softened, he felt compelled. He turned to Ryan and Damien, then back towards Javi.

"Very well, the Vanir gods will aid you in this mission."

Javi smiled, almost in disbelief that Njord actually agreed to help. When they last talked, they were not on good terms. This was a step in the right direction.

"Fantastic," Javi exclaimed, "Let's get our weapons and armor, gather our strength, and meet back in the realm travel room tomorrow." Njord nodded his head and left the throne room, followed by Ryan and Daniel to return to Vanaheim. The court of Asgard stood from their thrones and began to walk to their rooms, except for Tyr, who went back to the party to break the news to Aegir. As Javi walked to his room, Fiora ran up to him and grabbed his hand.

"I'm not going to be able to convince you to stay here, am I?" Javi asked.

Fiora shook her head, "Not a chance, this is just as much my responsibility as it is yours."

Javi loved Fiora's morality. It typically put her in dangerous situations, but after she fought in Jotunheim he had complete faith that she could handle herself. Often times, it was Fiora who worried more for Javi. "Javi," she started, "Are you sure this is the best possible plan, to bring all of us down there? That would leave our realms unguarded."

"The Valkyrie will stay here then, just us and the Vanir."

Fiora lowered her head, "I just have a feeling that this is going to be a lot different than how things were with Ymir."

Javi nodded his head, "It will be, that's why we'll be careful."

Pleased with his answer, Fiora let go of his hand and kissed his cheek. "Thank you, Javi," she said. With that, she bid him good night and went to her own room to prepare. Javi did the same.

Once he had all of his armor set up in the far side of his room, Javi sat down on his bed, thinking of every possibility the next few days could provide. When he was giving the orders, he had felt incredibly confident in the powers that were on his side. However, as he sat there contemplating, one thing Njord said kept bothering him. He said that

Hel was stronger than all of them combined. For a moment, he felt that perhaps he was in over his head.

He stood and walked to the tree that stood in the center of his room. Hanging from it was the golden armor he wore when he fought the stone dragon in Svartalfheim. In the midsection of the armor were three gaping holes. It was where the dragon had struck him. Javi touched his stomach, he could still feel the scars through his tunic. He remembered how weak he felt in that fight, how ineffective his weapon was. The thought that he would be facing a threat even greater than that almost daunted him, but just as quickly as it came, his fear subsided.

He wasn't where he was before. He was stronger, faster, and smarter, just like everyone else. They all had grown so much since they first accepted the responsibility that was passed onto them. If they made it this far, they could make it through what they would face in the mortal realm.

Javi walked back to his bed and sat down. He knew that in this mission, the danger was inevitable. Every second they spent finding Hel was one in which her power would be taking moments away from their life, literally. The mission was urgent, and they were on the clock, but in knowing this, Javi still had faith. They could save Midgard, and as long as they fought together, nothing would be able to stop them.

Modi looked to the sky and breathed deeply as he sat on the park bench. Though he couldn't see them, he could feel their motives. He knew that they were coming, his plan was falling into place. As he sat there silently celebrating, he felt the presence of another who was standing behind him.

"Hello Magni," he said, "It would seem that our game has begun."

Magni, the second son of Thor, had been waiting on the sidelines as his brother Modi weaved his plan together like a web. However, Magni wasn't one for waiting, and his patience was wearing thin. "How could you be so certain that she will eliminate all of them," he demanded to know.

Modi's grip tightened on his wooden staff. "I'm not certain of that, I'm certain that she will weaken them."

"Why must we weaken them first," Magni asked, "We could kill them all ourselves if we so desired."

Modi sighed, "So zealous, yet so short-sighted." Magni frowned at the insult. Modi continued, "We can hurt them, yes, but if Hel carries no disdain for them, it is inevitable that they will return." That's what Modi was worried about. He feared that the actions he took would not be permanent. If he was to kill them, he wanted their souls to remain in Helheim. If Hel could see to that, then it would be so.

Magni finally understood, "You put them against each other so that hatred would be birthed from their battles." Modi shook his head and Magni smiled. "You have grown wise Modi, the game has begun indeed."

CHAPTER SEVEN: THE

FEAR OF DEATH

Njord had not slept well that night. Quite frankly, none of the Vanir slept well but Njord and his daughter Freyja slept the worst of all. None of the reborn gods knew how powerful Hel was, but Njord remembered. It happened shortly after the Aesir and Vanir war, while Njord was forced to reside in Asgard.

Odin, followed by the rest of the Aesir gods, set out to capture three of Loki's children. The giant serpent Jormungandr, the giant wolf Fenrir, and the Goddess of Death Hel were all brought to Asgard for Odin to judge. He cast Jormungandr into the oceans of Midgard first, as he deemed him too much of a threat. His eyes set upon Hel next. At first, he decided to keep her in Asgard for a time, as he wanted to strengthen the Aesir tribe of gods. Before long, his plan backfired.

Hel's power manifested in the form of black smoke, and the older she got, the more potent that power became. What made it worse was that she couldn't control it. Before long, her darkness covered the entirety of Asgard and caused every god that resided within to fall deathly ill, including Njord and Freyja.

Odin had no choice but to cast her out of Asgard. So against Loki's plea for his daughter, he banished her to Niflheim, a realm within Helheim, and declared her to be the goddess of the unworthy dead. Her power soaked the realm so deeply, no living thing would be able to reside there for long.

Njord remembered how he had nearly died during that time. The very air he breathed choked him. Now, he was supposed to go into a realm where something very similar was happening. He was not excited, to say the least. If any of them were to stay in Midgard for too long, they would not be returning home. However, Njord knew that he could not say no, it was his sworn duty to protect those who could not. He had to help Javi find Hel, and return her to Niflheim.

His mind made, Njord put on his shining cobalt blue armor and went to Freyja's room in the marble castle to see if she was ready to go. When he got there, he could see that she was fully dressed in her green armor and ready to go. However, there was a fear in her eyes that Njord knew too well.

"Good morning daughter, ready to go," he asked her. Freyja looked up at him, tears welled up in her eyes.

"Why are we following these children, father," she asked in return, "They do not know the danger that lies in the journey ahead.

Njord sat on the bed next to Freyja, "No, no they don't."

"Then why are we helping them, putting our lives in danger because they said so?"

Njord sighed, "Because it is the right thing to do." Freyja looked at her father shocked. "I know that in the old age, we were not so much concerned with the wellbeing of mortal lives, but you and I

both know that times have changed."

Silent tears fell from Freyja's eyes, the

nightmares of Hel in the Old Age plagued her mind.

She was not at all ready to face her again, even

though it had been eons since she last saw her.

Truth be told, none of the gods in that time were too

keen on crossing paths with Hel ever since she was

thrown into Niflheim.

Njord saw the fear in Freyja's eyes, and

though his eye's shared the same fear, he wrapped

his arm around her and gave her a warm,

comforting hug. "Everything is going to be alright."

Just then, Felix (Freyja's reincarnated

brother, Freyr), walked into the room. Like his

father, he had the intention to make sure his sister

was okay. When he saw Njord already there, he turned to walk back towards the realm travel room to go to Asgard. However, Njord saw him, and with his heart full of love, he asked his son to come and take a seat next to him.

Felix sat on the bed and Njord put his other arm around him. Felix smiled, "You know, I'm actually pretty excited about this."

Njord chuckled, "How so?"

"Well, considering that I missed out on fighting Ymir, this is going to be my first legit mission!"

Njord furrowed his brow, "Legit?" It then occurred to Felix that Njord still spoke in a mostly old fashioned way. Words like legit or dope sounded like gibberish to him. "Legit as in actually real," Felix explained.

Njord chuckled, "Oh, well I wouldn't say that. Aiding the Elves in rebuilding Alfheim was absolutely a real mission."

"No, I mean now I actually get to draw my sword," Felix replied, "Use the battle magic the Freyja taught me."

Njord faked a smile. He disapproved of Felix's enthusiasm for going to Midgard, but he wanted him to stay as optimistic as possible. Instead of voicing his own worries and doubts, Njord rubbed the brown curly hair on Felix's head and said, "Let us gather the others, it's time to go."

The trio finished putting on their armor and swords, then grabbed Ryan and Daniel as they headed to their own realm travel room. The Vanir tribe of the gods walked through the portal that led to Asgard, immediately joining the Aesir, who was waiting for them in Asgard's realm travel room already. After sharing very brief pleasantries Javi stepped in the middle of all of them, wearing his black stone dragon scale armor. He cleared his throat, prepared to give the mission plan.

"As good as it is to see everyone again, we have no time to hang out. Every second down in Midgard, someone is falling victim to Hel's power. We all have our weapons, our armor. and our strength, it's time to go. We will split into four teams, three on land and one patrolling the ocean." As nervous as Njord was, the god of the sea smiled at the notion of once again sailing the ocean. He couldn't remember the last time he had a decent

venture out on the open sea.

Javi noticed Njord's smirk, he made the right

decision, "Daniel was able to pinpoint the origin of

Hel's power near the east coast of North America,

possibly in the ocean. Njord, Daniel and Ryan will

take to the sea." Njord was irritated at first because

he couldn't sail alone, but having an all-seeing guy

and an invulnerable guy on his team was actually a

pretty good deal.

"Freyja, Felix and Tyr will take the center of

the east coast, Damien and Jacob will take the

north, Fiora and I, the south." Both nods of approval

and groans of annoyance emerged from the gods,

especially Damien, who did not enjoy traveling with

Jacob.

"We will completely cover our regions and meet back on the coast of North Carolina." Njord was impressed, Javi had orchestrated this plan by himself. He had grown since he had last seen him.

Once everyone grouped up, Daniel started to direct everyone through the portal leading to Midgard. His group would be the last to go through. Njord looked at the portal that shone through the wooden doorway and looked at the runes above it.

ᛗ ᛁ ᛝᚷ ᚨ ᚱᛝ

He had never been scared of runes before, but he was now because he knew where they would lead him. He had nearly died when Hel was in Asgard, and it didn't take long. He fought his own mind and tried to be optimistic, but he feared that he wouldn't walk back through. He feared he wasn't coming back.

Daniel grabbed his shoulder and shook him.

"You okay dude?" Njord didn't realize he was zoning out, which hadn't happened in years. He looked around and saw that everyone else had already gone through the portal.

"I'm sorry, is it time?" He asked.

"Yeah," Ryan spoke up, "It's our turn." Njord took a deep breath in, sweat was soaking his beard. Every step towards the portal felt like it took every bit of strength he had. His breath became heavy and weighed on his lungs.

"WAIT," Ryan shouted suddenly, "Does my invulnerability work on Hel's power?"

Njord turned and shook his head, "No one is invulnerable to death." He turned back to the portal, took a deep breath, and stepped through.

Njord was surrounded by the bright light of the Bifrost, shining in every color of the rainbow. However as that light dissipated, his eyes were met with the darkness that had befallen Midgard. Ryan and Daniel appeared in the realm behind Njord. Their once magical and luminescent armor suddenly turned into regular mortal clothing. They would still perform their protective duties, but dwarven magic hid their true form.

As they stood on the beach that the Bifrost had brought them to, they looked upon what Hel had done to the realm. "Woah," Ryan said, "This place really did go to crap." He was right. Though they were on the shore facing the ocean, they could

see how badly Hel's power damaged Earth. It was

dark as night and pitch black clouds completely

covered the sky. Fog completely enveloped them,

and it carried a strange but unmistakable scent, the

scent of death.

All three of the gods standing there

immediately felt weakened. Their movements felt

stiff and their breaths became heavy. "We don't

have much time," Njord said, "We have to go now."

While it had been a long time, Njord still had the

powers that came with being the god of the sea. He

could sense he was standing in front of the Atlantic

Ocean, facing towards the direction of North

America. In mortal sea vessels, the journey would

take weeks, months even. But Njord's vessel was far from mortal.

He walked into the water in front of him and went waist-deep. He put the palms of his hands on the surface of the water. "Come back to me darling," he whispered to the depths of the sea. At first, nothing happened, and Ryan and Daniel looked at him like he was insane. Then in the distance, the water started to rumble and ripple in the distance. Every second the rumbling became more and more intense, something large was emerging from the depths.

Suddenly, the surface of the water broke, and something big and white came to rest upon the surface. Ryan and Daniel stopped looking at Njord and stared with mouths wide open at what they realized to be a beautiful Viking longship with golden sails. On the bow hung the skull of a dragon and the stern had a tail that curled into a spiral.

Njord looked at the longboat with pride in his eyes, the sails illuminated some of the darkness surrounding it and warmed his heart. He looked back at Daniel and Ryan, who now felt terrible for thinking Njord had become a psychopath. He grinned and said, "All hands on deck."

CHAPTER EIGHT: THE LIVES YOU SAVE

Javi did expect to get sick, but not this quickly. As he was throwing up in a nearby brush, Fiora was waiting for him, leaning on a nearby tree. After his stomach finally recovered, Javi stood back up, grabbed his spear (Which now appeared to be an umbrella) and walked weakly back to her side. "We gotta hurry," he said, "People aren't gonna last long here."

Fiora stood up straight, "Javi, we aren't going to last long here. We haven't even been here for five minutes and we are already sick."

Javi shook off the chills that covered his body, "Okay, let's keep moving." Though Javi knew they were in the south, he didn't know where north

was, and that's where they needed to go. However,

Javi had prepared for a moment such as this. After

Jotunheim, he learned that he lacked directional

capabilities when it came to getting somewhere, so

he had the Elves give him something that would be

able to help. He turned his wrist so that it faced him,

and looked at the golden tattoo that was etched on

the inside of his forearm.

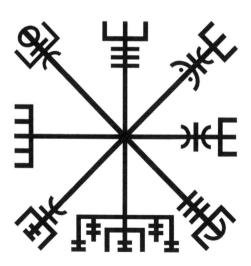

Vegvisir, that's what it was called. Its magic made it so that the bearer would not ever get lost. Javi took a deep breath and held his destination in mind. The runic stave suddenly glowed brightly, stinging his arm slightly. The power within the stave coursed through Javi's body, his veins began to glow and following soon after his eye. Suddenly, directions started to bounce around his mind, like a map was being downloaded into his brain. Every turn to take, every road, every obstacle. He knew where he had to go. The magic of the stave began to diminish and the glowing parts of his body returned to normal.

"That is so cool," Fiora chuckled, "So where to?"

Javi turned left and said, "This way, I'll let you know when we need to turn." Javi started walking, but Fiora grabbed his wrist and pulled him towards her.

"Hey uh, I know I shouldn't think like this but considering how dangerous this mission is, I just wanna say…"

Javi interrupted her, "Fiora, I already know what you're about to say. Please don't keep thinking like that."

"How do we not think like that?" She said sorrowfully, "I know I should try to be optimistic, but we are facing up against the goddess of death herself." She paused for a moment, not wanting to fill Javi's ears with negativity, nor did she want that negativity falling upon her as well. She took a deep breath and said, "Whatever happens, just know that I love you... with all of my heart, I love you."

Javi looked into her one green eye as she looked into his. "I love you too Fiora." She smiled and thought about kissing him, but they had already spent too much time standing in one spot.

"Let's go ahead and get moving before you throw up again."

Javi chuckled, "Good idea," He began to walk towards the direction that Vegvisir pointed him to, but then turned back to Fiora, "Is it okay if I eat an Idunn Apple now?" The magical apples that grew in the center in the garden of Asgard possed magical properties. It gave the gods strength when they were weak and preserved their youthful appearance. Every group had four apples and Javi felt like he could really use one, his strength was in the dumps.

Fiora took the leather bag she brought from Asgard off of her back and took one of the Idunn Apples that she had packed in case either of them needed it. "Here you go," She said as she handed the apple to Javi. Javi grabbed the apple and took a huge bite out of it. Javi could never get used to how good Idunn Apples tasted. It was as crisp as an apple could get and as he chewed it, it turned into honey in his mouth.

Immediately, Javi felt like he had a new body. His strength was restored and his stomach didn't feel like it had turned upside down. "Thanks, hon," He said to Fiora.

"You are very welcome."

They began to walk in the direction that Vegvisir had instructed them to. The further they walked through the woods, the more uneasy the both of them felt. Fiora was new to the feeling, but Javi knew it well. It was that same feeling that he had when he was running through the woods with his wolves. When he encountered a Draugr, the intelligent living dead warriors that plagued the earth. Javi's grip righted on his disguised weapon and it turned back into the spear, Gungnir.

Fiora noticed, "What's wrong? You see something?"

Javi shook his head, "Not yet, but be on guard." Fiora reached into the pocket of her ripped jeans and pulled out a stick of lipstick. Her grip righted on it and it quickly transformed into a glowing red sword.

Javi and Fiora walked quickly, but cautiously, both feeling that someone, somewhere, was following them. All Javi wanted to do was get to the city just outside of the forest. They were close, but not nearly close enough to feel safe. Suddenly there was a smell that smacked Javi and Fiora in the face violently.

"Ugh, what *is* that," she said rhetorically. Javi knew she wasn't expecting an answer, but he knew he could provide one. The smell was potent, pungent and putrid. It smelled just like that living dead warrior that attacked Javi in the woods before he knew he was a god, just much stronger, which meant there was more than one.

"Get ready to fight," Javi warned, "We are being followed by Draugr." As soon as he said it, the pungent smell of death intensified, and through the shrubs and bushes surrounding them, a dozen of the living dead revealed themselves, weapons drawn and ready to attack. The Draugr with glowing yellow eyes in front of Javi walked closer than all the others, but still a considerable distance away. He was wearing a rotten leather tunic and an old bronze metal helmet.

"And here I thought finding the rulers of Asgard would be difficult." He said with a raspy and gurgling voice, "You fell right into her trap."

It didn't take a genius to know that the Draugr was talking about Hel, which meant that she knew they were here. If this was truly a trap, they had made a grave mistake coming to Midgard.

Javi stepped forward and positioned his spear to attack, the Draugr followed immediately after. Fiora stepped in front of Javi, grabbed his wrist and pushed his arm back down. "What does she want, why is she poisoning the earth," she asked the lead Draugr.

The Draugr laughed a deep gurgling laugh and said, "Now why would I tell you that?" As soon as that last syllable left his mouth, he pointed his sword towards Fiora and Javi and in response, the Draugr surrounding them rushed in to attack.

Javi and Fiora spared no time in defending against the attacks, while also providing their own. Fiora gracefully dodged the spear thrusts and sword slashes from three of the Draugr with grace. After rendering their guard open, she swung her sword towards them with such power, it cut them all down like grass.

Javi remembered the ring that Brokkr gave him and put his hand out like he was holding a shield and just as soon as he did, the round golden shield appeared in fabulous golden light. As soon as it formed, the sword of a Draugr clashed against it and shattered into pieces. Javi and the Draugr both looked down and the shattered pieces of iron on the ground. The Draugr looked horrified, but Javi was looking at them in pride. While the Draugr was still staring at his broken sword, Javi sliced him in half with the tip of Gungnir and black ooze spouted from its wounds. Javi's eye turned golden and he began to fight against all the other Draugr that came against him.

In no time Fiora and Javi destroyed the eleven Draugr. When the last one disappeared in a smelly green mist, they turned their attention on the one who was leading them. The Draugr smiled, showing proudly what remained of his teeth.

"Who are you," Fiora demanded.

"In life, I was known as Aleksander," he said, "Now I am merely a shadow of who I once was."

"I will only ask you one more time," Javi growled, "What do you want."

"Boy," Aleksander scoffed, "You threaten a dead man who has nothing to lose, and we already have what we came for."

"We didn't give you anything," Javi replied.

"But aye, you did. Your location and knowledge of your power." Javi's heart dropped. They weren't there to kill them, they were there to find out where they were and what they could do. It was a battle strategy, Hel was learning about her enemy. "The lives you save now does not atone for what you did before. We will meet again soon, Allfather, all of us."

Javi threw his spear at Aleksander, but just before it hit him, Aleksander disappeared in a swirl of green mist. Realizing his attempted attack was pointless, Javi stuck out his hand and called the spear back to his grasp.

He turned to Fiora and uttered with fear in his voice, "We have to move, *now*."

CHAPTER NINE: MR. BOOT

"This is officially the worst mission ever," Jacob had been complaining the entire walk, and it had only been a few hours. Damien was trying his best not to cave in Jacob's chest with Mjolnir, which currently looked like a silver hydro flask. Being brought up as rough as he was, it hurt his pride he was paired with someone who complained about their feet hurting, or how dark it was the entire journey. The only thing Damien saw worthy of the complaint was the fact that both he and Jacob were sick as dogs. Whatever Hel had done really was screwing with them. If they were there for too long, things weren't going to end well for them.

"Let's just hurry up and get this done," he grunted, trying his best to be civil. Jacob picked up on Damien's attitude and thought about ways to lighten the mood.

In all honesty, the mood needed to be lightened everywhere. The darkness covering the Earth was ruining everything. It really did look like the end of the world. Jacob thought about that for a moment. The only ones standing between the apocalypse and life was him and his friends. He really did have to take this mission more seriously.

He resisted the urge to pull a prank on Damien (even though he really wanted to do one) and looked for ways to help them navigate. Finding Hel was going to take a lot more than wandering along the east coast, and it didn't help that Daniel still couldn't really see anything in the realm. They had no pointers, no guidance, no clues.

"This has to be the worst way to find Hel," Jacob sighed, "At this rate, we won't make it to the rendezvous point."

Damien was almost annoyed once again at the complaint, but Jacob was right. This plan definitely needed a bit more planning. "You have any ideas," he asked him.

Jacob paused for a moment, Damien actually asked for his opinion, this was a historical moment! It sucked that he had to ask when Jacob didn't have any ideas whatsoever at the moment. If he had his way, everyone would all go back to Asgard and rethink their strategy. Jacob sighed and looked around the nearly empty streets of Albany.

Across the street from them, he saw an old Chinese restaurant. Jacob was never really a diehard fan of Chinese takeout, but he did know he was hungry and with a bit of trickery on his part, he was able to collect $30 from unsuspecting pedestrians. "We could think of something over lunch," he proposed to Damien. At first, Damien wondered why this was at all a good plan, but then the rumbling of his stomach drew his attention.

"You know what... good idea." Before five minutes were up, both of them were sitting at a table, stuffing their mouths with fried noodles and orange chicken.

Suddenly, Jacob's eyes looked up from his plate of food and straight at Damien. "Is it just me, or does it feel weird being back here?"

Damien's mouth was so full, you would think he wouldn't be able to utter a syllable through the mass of munched up food. Still, he was trying to find something to say. If he was going to be paired up with Jacob, it wouldn't hurt to try and be friendly. What better way to start than to have a nice, civilized conversation.

"Other than feeling like Sleipnir kicked me in the head, yeah, it does feel kind of funny." If he was really honest, "kind of" was a vast understatement. Being in Midgard almost didn't feel real, not because it was so spectacular, but because it was dull. The lack of magic and wonder they had come accustomed to simply wasn't there.

Jacob could see that Damien was still withholding what he really felt, but the fact he was talking to him was progress. "It's kind of sad, being here," He said, "I keep remembering the things that happened to me here, most of them weren't cool."

Damien looked at him curiously. What stuff would a guy like Jacob go through, couldn't be that bad, right? "What's your story man," he asked him.

"Nothing glamorous. I lived in an abusive foster home with two other kids. I pulled a prank that got my foster parents arrested, but in the process, I lost my two best friends. After that, I met Javi." Damien could tell there was more to the story, but he didn't want to push him to spill the beans. He could hear the grief in Jacob's voice when he was telling him just that bit. Damien was hard, but he wasn't heartless.

Jacob coughed (partially because he was starting to feel sickly again) and asked Damien, "What about you, where are you from."

"I don't know, I was born on the streets and raised by a homeless community. Learned how to fight when I was old enough to raise my hands to block," Damien paused and chuckled. If only all those that he fought knew that they were fighting against the god of thunder. "Going to Asgard was a no-brainer. Earth had nothing for me."

Jacob was speechless for once. Never would he have guessed that Damien had no home here. He wasn't the most eloquent guy, but he was well-spoken and most of the time, better behaved than Jacob. To think someone like him begged and fought for his food. What an upgrade this new life really was for him!

"Well I have an idea now," Jacob said, breaking the tension.

"Well, I'm all ears," Damien responded.

"We can search for the Hel from the sky." Damien laughed heartily.

"You do know I can't fly right. How are we getting into the sky."

Jacob's eyes glowed purple in anticipation, "Damien, I'm a shapeshifter! I'll change into a dragon or something, and you'll just come along for the ride!"

Damien sat back in his seat and crossed his arms. That was actually a really good idea. If done right, they could cover their region and then some in no time at all. "Alright, sounds good to me."

Jacob quickly paid the tab for their lunch break and the pair walked out of the restaurant. They started walking into a nearby alley to find a secluded place where Jacob could shapeshift, but Damien felt a twinge in his stomach that told him something was off.

The deeper they walked into the alleyway, the more they could hear the echo of their footsteps. However, Damien heard the rhythm of someone's footsteps that didn't match their own. They were being followed, and the twinge in Damien's stomach told him it wasn't just a regular person. A tall bearded man wearing a long brown hooded trench coat walking towards them at a much faster pace.

Damien gripped the hydro flask in his hand and it turned into the thunderous hammer Mjolnir. He turned around quickly, startling Jacob, and threw the hammer towards the stranger. To both Jacob and Damien, the hammer was flying faster than their eyes could see, but the stranger, he could see it. The leather boots on his feet began to glow in bright white light, and before Mjolnir struck him square in his chest, he dashed to the side, leaving behind a glowing white trail of footsteps behind him.

Upon realizing he missed, Damien recalled the hammer to his hand and prepared to throw it again, but the stranger held out his hand. "Please, I just wish to have a word."

"Who the hell are you," Damien demanded to know.

"I'd rather remain nameless to you, but you may call me Mr. Boot."

Jacob burst out laughing, Mr. Boot was an absolutely terrible substitute for a name. Mr. Boot turned his gaze towards Jacob and narrowed his eyes. Realizing that his chuckle may have just offended the stranger, Jacob stopped laughing and covered his mouth.

Mr. Boot turned back to Damien and asked, "Are you at all attributed to the darkness that covers this world?"

Damien looked at the man like he was speaking a foreign language, and Jacob realized that he had no idea what to say, so he spoke up. "No, but we are looking for the one who is, Hel."

Mr. Boot looked as if he was about to faint. "No," he whispered, "It is as I feared."

Impatient, Damien spoke, still wanting a straight answer, "Why are you following us!"

"I could tell you were different, that you were special." Damien stared at him, still ready to throw Mjolnir at a moment's notice. "The weapon you bear in your hands tell me I was right. So I ask you, who are you to be wielding Mjolnir?"

Jacob and Damien paused and started to connect the dots. This man was absolutely from the old age, they just didn't know who. All that was important to Jacob was that he wasn't hostile.

Jacob, himself being a trickster, could also tell who

tricksters were. He could tell Mr. Boot was an

honest man, whoever he was. He trusted him

enough to tell him who he was, "I am Jacob, this is

Damien. We have the spirits of Thor and Loki

inside of us."

"Just tell the man we are reincarnated Norse

gods," Damien groaned, "Stop being so fancy."

Jacob's eyes glowed purple, he was absolutely

going to pull a prank on him at some point in this

mission.

Mr. Boot looked at them first in disbelief,

until he saw Jacob's glowing eyes. He started to

walk forward and Damien instinctually rose Mjolnir

again.

"By the gods," Mr. Boot exclaimed, "Wyrd finally bends in our favor." Jacob and Damien looked at each other, confused at his statement. "If it is truly your quest to find the queen of the damned, then I will aid you." He stood in front of the pair of gods and stuck out his hand. Jacob, without a moment of hesitation, shook it.

"Let's go hunt a ghost!"

CHAPTER TEN: A GHOST IN THE WOODS

It was Felix's first time eating an Idunn Apple. He had never needed one before, mainly because he had yet to partake in a serious battle. Now, he absolutely needed something that could give him strength. Hel's power was already badly affecting them when he and Freyja first arrived, but it suddenly got so much worse, so much darker. Felix could barely see the apple he was eating, at least until Freyja lit her magic green fire on the ground between them.

"It must be nighttime," she said.

Tyr nodded his head in agreement, "There's no way to know where we are going. We have to wait until there is light."

The trio sat down on a fallen tree and looked into the green fire. Tyr and Freyja watched the magical sparks spew from the flame, dancing in the air.

Felix's attention however was on Freyja. Part of him was still in disbelief that she was his sister. He always wanted a sibling, but never did he think he would have a super old one. It was cool that she still looked young though, those Idunn apples really were the best anti-aging product. Freyja didn't look a day over 20, and she was incredibly beautiful. Felix wished he looked equally as handsome.

He closed his eyes and took a deep breath, the power of the golden apple was already restoring his strength. "Have you thought about the people here yet." Freyja at first said nothing, then nodded her head silently. Felix continued, "If this stuff is hurting us this bad, imagine what it's doing to regular people."

Freyja lowered her gaze, "It is likely that thousands have died already, which is why we need to find Hel as soon as possible."

Felix furrowed his brow, "So why are we just sitting here, Freyja?"

Tyr jumped into the conversation, "Can you see in this darkness Felix?"

Freyja nodded her head in agreement with Tyr's observation, "It is much too dark to travel a long distance right now.

"Freyja," Felix said with irritation in his voice, "You literally just created fire so we could see each other. Are you telling me you can't make a torch?"

Freyja sighed, "Felix, while this is a world for mortal beings, it is also shared with beasts of many kinds. Trolls, mare, Draugr, they all reside here. It is not smart for us to travel in the darkness knowing these creatures are roaming." Felix sat back frustrated, once again feeling like he was forced into being able to do nothing.

"Rest easy, brother," Freyja said soothingly, "We will leave at first light."

Felix started to lie down, but stopped, "You know what, I'll take first watch, you go ahead and rest first." Tyr was about to speak up in objection, but Freyja saw her brother's eyes and how much he wanted to help. She couldn't just say no to that.

"Very well. If something happens, wake me immediately." Felix nodded his head.

Freyja and Tyr laid their heads on the ground and in seconds, they had fallen asleep, but Felix waited a bit longer, just to be sure they weren't watching him, making sure that he stayed where he was. After ten minutes of waiting for any sign of consciousness, he could believe with absolute certainty that they were asleep. With that, he stood and walked into the woods. He held up his hand and called the magic of light into it, causing it to glow brightly, illuminating some of the darkness that was around him.

He wasn't planning on traveling far, he just wanted to check the perimeter around them. None of the gods knew where Hel was, so who was to say she was not in the woods with them. If that was so, he would find her, wake Freyja and Tyr, and the three of them would throw down with the goddess of death. To Felix, it sounded like a pretty good plan, but he doubted it would actually happen. He had a feeling if Hel was in the woods, she probably would have attacked them already. Either way, he wanted to do something that made him feel useful.

Suddenly, as he was walking through the trees, Felix noticed that it was somehow getting darker, and it was already pitch black. This darkness felt different, like it was able to pierce his heart. It was deep and it was terrifying. Felix brightened the magic in his hand to illuminate the forest a bit more.

Every step that he took felt wrong, as if his own legs knew that he was walking towards something he should have been walking away from. He felt weak and considered turning around to wake up the others, but he felt compelled to keep moving forward.

Left, right, left, right, his feet crunched the leaves beneath him in a rhythmic motion. Left, right, left, right, as much as he knew he should have been running away, he couldn't. Left, right, as soon as his right foot came in contact with the soft, cold forest floor, Felix froze. Chills began to run up his spine, towards the back of his neck, spreading out to all of his other limbs. He exhaled and saw his breath

rise in front of his mouth, though it was not cold.

He squinted his eyes and peered forward, there was

a figure of a girl standing a few yards away. Felix's

heart began to pound against his ribcage.

The girl standing there was wearing an outfit

similar to Freyja's, though he still couldn't tell

because her face was hidden. She wore ripped black

denim jeans, a black shirt, and a red plaid flannel.

"Freyja," Felix called out, "Is that you?" The figure

did not respond, which meant it was not a friend of

his. He tried to step backward, but when he

couldn't, he looked down. Hanging on to his ankles

where two rotting hands that emerged from the

ground. The girl quickly closed the distance

between her and Felix, and soon, they were face to face.

At this point, Felix was fully aware that this was not Freyja. It was a girl who was partially really pretty. The right side of her face was incredibly lush and full of life. She looked like she could have been a model if it wasn't for the left side of her face, which looked like a skull with grey skin. Both of her eyes were pitch black.

Felix took a deep breath and asked, "Are you Hel," his voice shook the whole time.

The girl grinned, "My name is Taliah, but yeah, you could say so."

At this point, Felix couldn't find any words to say. He was trapped by the goddess of death by herself, no words he could think of could save him.

He put his hand behind him and summoned sharp twigs and branches and turned them towards Taliah. The twigs and branches began to fly towards her as fast as bullets, and Felix smiled in pride, happy with his progress in magic.

His smile quickly diminished when the first twig flew through Taliah's head, yet she did not fall. It didn't even leave a mark, as if it passed through a ghost. The other twigs and branches followed soon after, but every single one passed through Taliah without leaving one mark. Her smile disappeared, and so did Felix's.

"Bad move," she said, her black eyes pierced his soul.

"What do you want with us," Felix asked with a shake in his voice, completely helpless to her.

She rose her finger and placed it on his lips, "Shhh." Black smoke started to leak from her hand and into Felix's nose. His breathing cut off and he began to choke on the air, the veins in his face turned black and began to circulate poison through his system.

"I want you to deliver a message for me. I want you to tell your friends that I am not hiding from them, they should be the ones hiding from me. I am coming for all of you, and none of your weapons can hurt me, even with all your strength." She pulled her hand away and all the smoke that went into Felix's body came back out through his nose. Felix gasped for air and filled his lungs with oxygen, falling to his knees. Taliah knelt down in front of him, "Don't try to run, I will find you, in any realm, in any world."

She stood to her feet and waved her hand over Felix. The rotten hands let go of his ankles and sunk back into the ground. "You have your message," she said, "Now deliver." Before Felix could beg or negotiate, she vanished in a swirl of black smoke. The forest immediately brightened and the trees became visible, though the sky was still dark.

Felix sat there on the ground, trying to process what just happened. The words that Taliah spoke echoed in his mind, he was in shock. Then slowly, the shock began to turn into terror. They were in her world, and she was coming after them.

Tears began to fall from his eyes, and his breathing

sped up. Then without a moment's notice, the terror

in his heart took over. He rushed to his feet and ran

through the forest, combing through the trees,

searching for his sister.

"FREYJA," he cried out, praying that he

wouldn't summon Hel back to the forest.

"FREYJA," he cried once more, "SHE'S HERE!"

CHAPTER ELEVEN: THE

WORLD SERPENT

Taliah sat on her makeshift throne of stone. It rested upon a mountain that overlooked a small city. She stared down at the moving lights within and began to cry. So many people were dying, not just in this city, but the entire earth. They were dying because of her power. However, as much as this hurt her, it also fueled her determination to complete her task.

The gods she had to kill were here, but they were spread out, and that was a problem. This meant Taliah would have to spend more time finding all of them rather than just taking them out all at once. The longer it took for her to kill them, the more innocent people would die. She wanted

nothing more at that moment than to remove her

power from the world, but she couldn't, not yet. Not

until all of the gods were dead.

Just then, the Draugr Aleksander approached

her and knelt down on one knee. "They are all here

and accounted for m'lady. What would you have us

do?"

Taliah sat and buried her face in her hands.

She wanted to raise up every Draugr in the country

to get them, but she had no idea how to do it. She

would have to think of something more tactical.

"Where are they all going," she asked Aleksander,

"If they are split up they have to regroup at some

point."

"They all seem to be heading towards one point on the eastern coast," he responded," The shore of a state you call Virginia."

Taliah smiled, they really did make this much easier than she thought it would be. "Set up a squad at their rendezvous point. The rest of you go and force them to get to the beach faster. If possible...kill them in the process."

⟨runic text⟩

As they traveled across the ocean, Ryan learned that he was most certainly *not* invulnerable to Hel's power. He also figured out that he had motion sickness, and both of those things were making his journey absolutely miserable. Almost every waking moment, he would vomit over the side of the ship.

After the first day sailing, Njord sent Ryan down below deck to try and help. It didn't really, but it let him be miserable by himself. Even though the room he was in was pitch black, he could still feel the rocking of the boat against the waves. He turned over on his side, hoping that he would be able to lessen the effect the rocking had on him.

Just then, Daniel walked into the room to check on his friend. "Hey buddy," he said, "How's everything going in here?"

Ryan turned his gaze towards Daniel and groaned. He felt like if he opened his mouth, a bunch of vomit would have flown out.

"I see," Daniel responded, trying not to laugh, "Well Njord said he was about to do something pretty cool."

Ryan sat up a little bit and quietly asked, "What's he going to do?"

"He's going to talk to Jormungandr, the World Serpent." Ryan's eyes widened. None of them had seen the world serpent before, at least not in this life. Ryan had only heard about it from Javi. It was one of the highly feared sons of Loki, so feared that Odin felt the need to cast him out of Asgard and into the oceans of Midgard. There, it grew so large it was able to wrap its body around the entirety of the world. The giant serpent was also Hel's biological brother. Perhaps in a way, they were still connected, if Jormungandr remembered who he was.

As weak as Ryan felt at the moment, he couldn't pass up the opportunity to see a living and breathing World Serpent. "Can I have an Idunn Apple," Ryan asked.

Daniel smiled, "Way ahead of you buddy." He turned his hand to reveal a glowing golden apple. He tossed it to him and Ryan reached out to catch it, but he couldn't move fast enough. The apple flew past his hand and smacked him square in the middle of his forehead. The apple bounced off and landed on the floor.

"Well, at least the apple doesn't hurt me." He reached down and grabbed the golden apple off of the floor, and took a bite out of it. Everyone else in Asgard seemed to like how the Idunn Apples tasted, but Ryan did not. The apple melted and turned into honey in his mouth, and Ryan was never truly fond of honey. Despite this the apple really did make him feel better. His stomach began to settle, his head began to hurt less. Ryan quickly finished eating the rest of the apple and stood up out of the bed, feeling like a new man.

"That's gonna buy you a good chunk of time without seasickness," Daniel said, "Let's go talk to a giant snake." Ryan got out the bed and started to walk out of the room until Daniel stopped him, "By the way, Njord said to grab your weapon. Jormungandr might be dangerous."

Ryan went to the foot of the bed he was lying on and grabbed the ax he had chosen as his weapon. Both Daniel and Ryan left the room and went up to the top deck. It was storming heavily, and lightning was streaking across the sky. Mountainous waves ran along the surface of the water, yet none of them came close to the boat. Njord was standing on the bow of the longship, staring into the waters below. "If you wish to see," he shouted to the boys, "Come and see."

Daniel and Ryan jogged to Njord and took out their weapons. "Where are we," Ryan asked Njord.

"In the Old Era," Njord responded, "Jormungandr's head rested in the place the mortals now call the Bermuda Triangle." Ryan was first shocked, but as he thought about it, he saw that it made sense in a way. Ships and planes that traveled over this spot supposedly disappeared without a trace. If Jormungandr's head was resting there, it was likely that they were in its stomach.

Njord turned to Ryan and stuck out his hand, "I need your ax."

Ryan gripped his ax tightly, "Why do you need it."

"If Jormungandr's head lies here, it is likely that he is asleep, and unfortunately there is seldom that can wake him."

"So you are going to throw an ax at him," Ryan exclaimed.

Njord nodded his head, "If thrown hard enough, it'll seem more like a push and hopefully, that will wake him."

Daniel stepped forward, "This doesn't seem like the most thought out plan, would he even be alive?"

Njord sighed, "It's just a theory, if you all have returned from the dead, then it is likely he has too."

"And throwing an ax at him is the best way to wake him?"

Njord rolled his eyes, "Look, I do not know what the best plan is for this. None of us besides Thor have actively looked to find Jormungandr. I'm in uncharted territory here too, but if anyone knows where Hel might be it's him."

After a moment of hesitation, Ryan stepped forward and handed Njord the ax. "Well it's now or never." Njord grabbed the ax and stepped on the edge of the bow. He stared into the water and wishing with all of his heart that fate would guide his hand. He stuck out his free hand towards the water and took a deep breath. His eyes began to glow in a green and blue color, the same color illuminating his hand. Suddenly, the water began to react.

Not too far from the longship, the surface of the water began to swirl. "Um Njord," Daniel said, shocked at what he was seeing, "This isn't going to take us under the water right?"

"Not if you let me focus," Njord responded without turning around. The swirl in the water was getting larger very quickly and soon, the longship was sitting on the edge of it. At this point, both Ryan and Daniel knew what Njord was doing. He was making a maelstrom, a giant whirlpool in the water. The longship got caught in the current of the whirlpool and began to orbit around its epicenter.

Ryan and Daniel fell down on the deck, frantically searching for something to hold on to. Even if there weren't going under the water, it was nearly impossible for them to keep their balance. However, the speed at which the boat was moving did not seem to bother Njord at all. He stood firmly on the edge of the boat, one hand holding the ax to the sky, on hand outstretched towards the water fueling the whirlpool. The only light came from Njord's eyes and the lightning streaking across the clouds.

Njord then flexed every muscle he had in the arm holding the ax, and in one fantastic thrust, he cast it into the sea. He lowered the arm that was stretched out to the water, and the whirlpool subsided. His eyes returned back to their normal blue-green shade. Ryan and Daniel stood back up and walked to the edge of the bow beside Njord. After waiting several seconds, Ryan spoke up, "Um, I don't think it worked."

"Patience," Njord responded. He stared into the waters, waiting for a movement, a sound, anything that told him that his plan worked, that Jormungandr was risen and alive. After nearly 2 minutes of staring at the water, Njord sighed and turned around, "Recall you ax Ryan."

Ryan could see that Njord was let down. That was the best shot they had at finding Hel, which meant the chances of her being found were all but none. Disappointed, Ryan held out his hand and in a few seconds, the ax flew out of the water and into his grasp. He looked into the darkness of the ocean one last time. His eyes widened we he saw that the surface of the water looked like it was boiling.

"Uh guys," Ryan shouted to Njord and Daniel, who was walking away, "I think something's happening."

Something was happening indeed. The deck of the longship began to shake as if there was an earthquake taking place within the ocean. Njord and Daniel ran to the edge of the boat and looked into the water. As soon as they did, an enormous rumbling sound emerged from the depths of the sea.

Then they saw it. A short distance away, Jormungandr was emerging from the surface of the water, and it was a thousand times as large as Ryan and Daniel thought it was. It seemed as if a mountain covered in barnacles was rising out of the ocean. It quickly towered over the longship, and its head wasn't even completely out of the water. After several seconds of the giant serpent rising from the water, they finally saw its giant shining purple eyes staring at them.

Compared to Jormungandr, the longship that they were standing on would be the smallest crumb. The beast opened its mouth, exposing two giant fangs and hundreds of other rows of sharp teeth. It let out a deafening roar, forcing Njord, Daniel, and Ryan to cover their ears.

"Njord," Ryan shouted, "He doesn't sound happy!"

"He sounds pissed," Daniel exclaimed.

"Hold on," Njord shouted. He held his hand towards Jormungandr. His eyes glowed blue and as he opened his mouth and spoke in a tongue that neither Ryan or Daniel understood. "FRITH," he shouted at the top of his lungs, hoping the magic he was using would allow Jormungandr to hear him, "FRITH!"

The serpent stopped roaring and looked at Njord with suspicion in his eyes. It began to bellow out a deep and loud groan, moving its mouth as if it were forming words. Though more drawn out, it sounded similar to whatever language Njord was speaking.

"Is that thing talking," Ryan yelled.

"Yes," Njord responded, "He remembers everything that happened in the Old Age. He still blames us for his death before." Njord turned his attention back towards Jormungandr. He spoke more in that mysterious language, something that Ryan and Daniel felt to be an apology. The giant serpent looked towards them, its reptilian eyes still showing signs of suspicion. It opened its mouth and bellowed out a few more words.

"What's it saying," Daniel shouted.

"He still carries mistrust." Njord responded, "But I promised him that we won't cause him any harm."

"Ask, him about Hel," Ryan yelled.

"I'm getting to that." Njord turned back towards Jormungandr and began to speak, but the giant beat interjected. It bellowed more of those long drawn out words and turned its head towards the sky. Njord turned to Daniel and Ryan, "It's asking if we are here to save this world."

Njord looked at Jormungandr and began to speak once again, the serpent was listening intently. After Njord finished talking, Jormungandr slowly turned its mountain-sized head towards the sky. Its giant purple reptilian eyes peered into the dark clouds that lingered above them. Jormungandr closed its eyes for a few moments, then turned towards the longship again.

Once again, the giant serpent bellowed a few more words. "He agreed to help up find Hel, but after we finish our business here, he requests that we leave Midgard immediately."

"We have no problem with that," Ryan said, "Asgard is way better."

Njord smiled and turned back towards Jormungandr and asked for Hel's location in that strange language. Jormungandr thought for a moment, then bellowed his answer towards the trio standing in the boat.

"It has been some time since he last checked," Njord translated, "But Jormungandr recalls feeling her presence in the place the mortals call, Florida."

CHAPTER TWELVE: WE WERE SISTERS ONCE

"Javi," Fiora exclaimed, "Just admit that this was a terribly thought out plan!" After a day and a half of wandering through cities, trying to blend in with the crowd, both Javi and Fiora were doubtful they would ever find Hel. They were getting sicker and sicker, it would only be a matter of time before it became fatal. They had no idea what to look for, no clues or coordinates. Their hope began to dwindle.

"What else were we supposed to do Fiora," Javi snapped, "Sit up in Asgard while everyone else here died?"

Fiora's already mad face turned into an intense glare, "That's not what I'm saying," she yelled, "I'm saying we should have made a plan, a better one than *wander and hope*."

"Well, it's too late now!" Javi had not been this mad in a long time. He regretted yelling at Fiora but trying to shove it in his face that he messed up was not going to make anything any better. As they sat in silence in that alleyway trying to figure out where they would go, Javi realized something, he was afraid. He was afraid of Hel, afraid of what she would do, afraid that he brought everyone he cared about on a suicide mission. He fought a war in his mind trying not to let that fear cloud his judgment.

"Fiora," he whispered, I don't think I can do this."

"What do you mean?"

"Defeating Hel, I don't think I can do it." He shook his head, feeling nothing but contempt for himself, "I feel like we did exactly what she wanted us to."

"Javi," Fiora said, feeling bad for yelling at him before, "Don't say that, there's still hope."

"I'm sorry, but I'm not seeing hope Fiora. Both of us are already sick, and we have a week-long journey ahead of us if we want to cover this whole region," Javi's head hung low, "We will not survive that journey."

As much as she wanted to hear Javi be his optimistic self, Fiora knew he was right. If they stuck with what they were doing now, none of them would make it. There had to be another way. "What do you think we should do," Fiora asked softly.

"We have to get to the rendezvous point," Javi instructed. He was about to consider the length of time it would take to get there if they walked, but then he remembered something that he had forgotten for a long time. "I'm a shapeshifter," he whispered at first to himself.

"Wait," Fiora interjected, "What did you say?"

"I can shapeshift," Javi said louder, almost yelling, "I'm not as good at is as Jacob, but I can still do it."

Fiora jumped to her feet in joy, "Well what are we waiting for, let's do…"

Neither of them saw it coming, nor did they hear anything that could have hinted to it. Fiora fell down to her side, a black spear lodged into her side.

"FIORA," Javi shouted as he rushed towards his fallen lover. She groaned in pain, the spear hit mere inches below where her lungs were. "Stay with me Fiora," Javi exclaimed, "Everything is going to be okay."

A chuckle emerged from the distance, and two glowing yellow eyes peered through the darkness, "Do not make a promise you cannot keep Allfather." The Draugr Aleksander was approaching them, and he appeared to be alone.

"Why," Javi pleaded, "Why would you do this?"

Aleksander stopped walking, "In the old age I pledged my life to you. I yearned to fight by your side when the day of Ragnorak came."

The smell of the Draugr was starting to make Javi sick, "Then why are you fighting us?"

"Because you abandoned me," Aleksander growled through his rotten teeth, "I fought gloriously on the battlefield, and when it came time for me to fall, I fell with a sword in my hand." Aleksander sounded as if he was close to tears, "But when my eyes opened again, I didn't awake in the halls of Valhalla, I awoke in the cold embrace of Niflheim. You didn't even seem me worthy enough for Helheim. In death, all I've yearned for was to harm you."

Javi felt bad for him, but he didn't much care for him. Fiora's movement began to slow and the only thing keeping her from bleeding out was the spear lodged in her ribcage that Javi so badly wanted to remove.

Though he was not wounded, he could feel her pain. Knowing that he wasn't prepared and that he failed to protect her tortured him. He didn't care about Aleksander's sad story, he wanted to kill him.

As anger blinded his rationality, Javi rushed to his feet and armed himself with Gungnir. He launched at Aleksander, who was unmoved by Javi's decision to fight. He had a trick of his own up his sleeve.

Javi didn't know how it happened, but when it happened, it was much too late to respond. Just as he was about to thrust his spear into the Draugr's head, a swarm of dark black smoke surrounded him, instantly weakening him. He fell to the ground inches in front of Aleksander, who had not let his smile fall.

Aleksander knelt in front of Javi and sighed, almost as if he pitied him. "I want to kill you, Odin," he said as a cloud of black smoke appeared, "But that is not my destiny."

"It's mine," a girl's voice spoke through the smoky wall. Aleksander disappeared in a swirl of green smoke and a girl stepped out of the darkness and walked towards Javi, who immediately knew who he was talking to. The telltale sign was her face, half alive and half dead. "I got to say, I expected this to be a lot harder. I mean, you are the Allfather, one of the most powerful gods."

Javi writhed in pain, his whole body felt like it was on fire. "W-why," he said weakly, "What did we do?"

"It's not what you did," Taliah said, "It's what you can do." Even in his dying eyes, Javi was visibly confused. As far as he could remember, he harbored no will to do anyone wrong. Taliah saw his puzzled gaze, "You ended the world already before. It rebuilt itself, but so have you and all the other gods. I can't let you end the world again."

Suddenly a scream emerged within the alleyway and both Javi and Taliah looked towards its source. It was Fiora, who had just pulled the spear out of her side and placed her hands on the wound. With her eyes glowing red, a bright light appeared where the wound was. Fiora was using magic to heal herself.

As Fiora repaired the damage done by Aleksander's spear, Taliah's eyes widened. Fiora struggled to her feet and looked towards the girl kneeling in front of Javi, "No… it can't be."

"Fiora… oh no…" The two girls stood staring at each other in shock. Fiora looked at Javi as he lay motionless on the ground, tears began to well up in her eyes.

"Let. Him. Go, Taliah," she demanded.

"I'm sorry, but I can't do that. I have to do this."

"NO," Fiora cried out as she marched towards Taliah, "You don't know who you are hurting Taliah, let him go now!"

"I know who I'm killing Fiora, I'm killing Odin, the one who made almost slaughtered the entire universe. It's my mission Fiora, as much as I hate doing it. I'm doing what it takes to save the world."

Fiora's eyes turned fiery red, "By doing what! You are killing everyone Taliah! This isn't saving the world!" Tears began to fall from Taliah eyes as they turned pitch black, "Never in a million years did I think you could be so evil."

Anger, guilt and shame ran through Taliah's veins, "You don't understand, as long as the gods live, the entire universe is at risk. Every moment that my power surrounds the Earth hurts me, but this is for the greater good."

At this point, Taliah and Fiora both had tears streaming from their eyes. "I'm sorry Fiora, but this has to be done."

Fiora wiped the tears from her eyes. All she wanted was to see Javi freed from the power of death that kept him on the ground, "Taliah, you can't possibly believe that."

The goddess of death nodded her head and held out her hand, "Join me Fiora, we can do this together, and you'll see. After this is done, me and you can rule over a free universe." Fiora stared at the hand reaching out to her. Those hands killed so many people, those hands were hurting the love of her life. Taliah saw the hostility in Fiora's eyes,

"Please Fiora, I don't want to have to hurt you. We were sisters once."

"*Once* Taliah, I don't know who you are anymore." Fear, anger, and resentment flowed through her veins. Her eyes were never so brightly red before. She drew her sword, her heart not wanting to harm Taliah, her mind all too willing.

"Don't make me kill you," Taliah begged, "Please." It was at this moment that both of them realized they had been arguing so much, they had not paid any attention to Javi, who was now standing to his feet, despite being surrounded by Taliah's power. His one eye was glowing so bright, both of them were forced to shield their eyes. Javi rose his golden glowing spear into the air, the spirit of battle surging through his body and the metal of Gungnir.

Before Taliah could answer back with an attack of her own, Javi grasped the spear in both hands and brought it to the ground. As soon as the tip of the spear came in contact with the ground, the ground surrounding him shattered and all of the energy inside of him rushed towards Taliah. She tried to teleport before it hit her, but it was much too late. The energy surrounded her and pushed her away from Javi at such a speed, she was barely visible to the naked eye. She crashed into a nearby building and broke the wall behind her. She fell to the ground motionless.

The darkness surrounding Javi disappeared and he fell on his back, weakened from the use of his power. Fiora rushed to him and tried to use her magic to strengthen them, there were no more Idunn Apples to be had. She held her hands over his head and tried to summon the magic, but it was to no avail. There was no power that could replace what Javi had given. He would have to wait for it to come back by itself.

Suddenly, as Fiora realized that her power was not helping, Javi began to realize something else entirely. The sky that was once covered in darkness began to clear up. The blue sky once again became visible, and sunlight once again shone upon the land.

"Look," Javi said as clearly as he could.

Fiora turned her gaze towards the sky and gasped. She had nearly forgotten what the world looked like without all of the death surrounding it. It was so beautiful, and a few seconds after, she realized that she didn't feel sick anymore. She felt strong, almost stronger than she felt in Asgard.

"Javi," she said with excitement in her voice, "I think you did it." But then she remembered the cost. Now that the anger had subsided and her rational thinking took control once again, she remembered Taliah. She looked up to where she had fallen, but she wasn't there.

Fiora wasn't sure what happened when one of them died. Did their bodies remain, did they disappear into dust or in a beautiful glowing light? She wasn't sure, but what she was certain about was that she was no longer there, and the sky was no longer dark.

Javi wasn't entirely sure what happened. He only felt an impulse that strong when he gave that speech in Jotunheim. He wanted to stand, but he didn't even have the energy to move his legs. "Just rest love," Fiora said, "Just rest for a little while." He didn't wait to be told twice. Javi closed his eyes, once again at peace. He saved lives, and he hoped that he had saved Midgard, but it was only a hope.

CHAPTER THIRTEEN: A

DARK IMPULSE

Taliah hobbled towards her stone throne, clutching her sides. So many questions were running through her head. How did that boy hurt her, what was that spear made of, what was she going to do next? However, there was one question that was louder than any other as she sat down, why was Fiora there?

She never thought that she would see her again, not after their parents divorced. Her mom, Theresa was given custody of Fiora, Noah was given custody of Taliah. It was mutual ground for the parents but for Taliah and Fiora, it was the worst thing that could happen. They were each other's comfort when Noah and Theresa started fighting. They showed each other compassion and understanding. Other than her mother, it was Fiora who made Taliah feel loved. Now, she was given the task to kill her.

"I can't," she cried, choking on her tears, "I can't do it!" It didn't matter if she was a goddess, it didn't matter if she was the most powerful one. Fiora was her sister, not even Modi could change that.

Aleksander walked up to Taliah's throne, "M'lady, are Odin and Frigg eliminated."

Taliah shook her head, "No, things got complicated."

Aleksander tilted his head, "Complicated? How could killing be complicated for the goddess of death."

"Odin was able to hurt me," She said, still grunting in pain, "He shot something out of his spear, and it hurt like hell."

"Magic," Aleksander whispered to himself.

"What," Taliah asked, "What did you say?"

"Magic," he said louder, "The only thing that can hurt you is pure magic."

"You didn't think that would be important for me to know," Taliah exclaimed.

Aleksander bowed his head, "I am sorry m'lady, I had assumed you had known of this weakness already."

Taliah sighed and looked up at the now clear sky. This was going to be more difficult than she thought. She needed a new plan fast. Then she realized, the sky was clear. Her mind had finally calmed enough for her to realize what was happening around her. The Asgardians think that they had won, they thought they saved the world. An idea was birthed into her head, one that she knew could work.

"It's okay Aleksander, but I have another job for you."

Aleksander smiled, thinking that he would finally get permission to battle Odin himself, "What is your will m'lady?"

"Pull your troops away from the gods, let them think that they have won." Aleksander's smile fell.

"What," he exclaimed, "But m'lady, they'll just go back to Asgard, and you have no access to the Bifrost to chase them there."

"They won't leave before meeting each other on the beach," Taliah said. She smiled, proud of herself for this plan. "There's only a few of them, but there will be thousands of us. Every single one of them will die Aleksander, everyone except for Fiora."

ᚠᛒᚲᛞᛗᚠᚷᚺᛁᛋᚠᛏᛗᛁᛉᚲᛇᚱᚺᛏᚾᚠᚠᚢᚾᛏ

After shapeshifting into a dragon, Jacob,

Damien and Mr. Boot quickly covered their region

and went on to go to the rendezvous point at the

beach. On the way, they found a distressed Fiora

and an unconscious Javi. After picking them up,

Jacob insisted that they go to the beach before

everyone's weight made him fall from the sky.

They arrived on the beach after nearly an hour after

sundown.

After everyone got off of his back, Jacob

immediately turned back into his normal form. He

was sweating and panting as if he had just run a

marathon. "That is the last time I play taxi driver for

you guys."

"Probably not," Damien teased, "Freyja,

Felix, and Tyr are still out there."

Jacob groaned, "They can walk!"

While the two bickered back and forth about whether or not to launch a rescue mission for the two Vanir siblings, Mr. Boot laid Javi down on the cold sand. Fiora knelt by his side. "It's going to be okay Javi, you're going to be okay."

Mr. Boot knelt beside Fiora and stared at Javi's face. "He's so young, but I can feel his spirit. Your love for each other is much deeper than it was before."

Fiora wiped tears from her eyes, "I know you want us to call you Mr. Boot, but I know you're a god. Who are you really?

Mr. Boot bowed his head and said, "I know should trust you, but now is not the time. When I am once again home in Asgard, I will tell you. It's

not safe for gods here."

"Why, mortals can't hurt us right?"

Mr. Boot shook his head and looked at

Damien, whose argument with Jacob was getting

more intense, "It's not the mortals Frigg, it's the

sons of Thor."

Fiora knew who he was talking about

immediately. They were the dreaded Magni and

Modi. After the battle in Jotunheim, Javi told her

about them. They were the monsters hiding under

the bed, someone that Fiora wished she would never

have to encounter. Having to chase Taliah around

made her forget that they were in Midgard too.

Mr. Boot continued, "They know you are

here, it was them who sent Hel after you. Even

uttering my name can put me at risk as well." Fiora

nodded her head, she understood. She looked

toward Javi again and ran her hand across his face.

In the middle of all this fuss and chaos, she wasn't

able to really spend the time with him that she

wanted to. Now, Javi wasn't able to do anything as

he lay motionless on the sand.

"Will he ever wake up," she asked.

Mr. Boot took a deep breath, "He exerted a

dangerous amount of power, so much that it exerted

his life force. Without the nectar of an Idunn Apple,

it is unlikely he will heal fully." Fiora was trying

her best to fight back the tears, but it wasn't

working. They streamed down her face.

Javi and Fiora had run out of the apples to

give. She fought to figure out where she could get

some, but then she remembered, every group had

their own bunch of Idunn Apples. It was possible

that Jacob and Damien still had Idunn Apples to

spare. She turned to them to ask if they did, but say

something that stole her breath first.

In the heat of their argument, Damien

pushed Jacob... hard. Jacob flew towards the water

and crashed into a shore break. Damien took out

Mjolnir and positioned to fight, "You don't know

me, Jacob," he yelled, tears stuck in his throat and

lightning flashing in his eyes, "We don't abandon

people, we don't abandon family!"

Jacob rose out of the water soaking wet, but

purple fire was still pouring through his skin.

"Family? None of you are my family, I'm not one

of you, I have never been." Jacob's eyes were

burning purple. "I'm not tied to any of you. If you get hurt, it means nothing to me." Damien rose Mjolnir to call down lightning upon Jacob, but before he could something cut off his thought process.

It felt like something was crawling through his mind, taking hold of his thoughts and destroying them. It didn't hurt, but Damien could tell that he couldn't control his body anymore. Unbeknownst to him, Jacob was using the Dark Elf mind trick that he had learned in Svartalfheim. Damien's eyes began to glow in the same shade of purple as Jacob's.

Fiora saw what was happening and ran towards Jacob. "NO," She cried, "Jacob, the Dokkalfar magic is taking over your mind, this isn't you." Jacob raised his hand and shot a giant plume of purple fire towards her.

It struck her so hard, she flew backward into the sand. Her head was throbbing and her ears were ringing Mr. Boot rose to respond, but another plume of fire was shot and held him down to the ground. "You all have forgotten," Jacob yelled, "I'm the god of mischief!"

He caused Damien to raise Mjolnir high into the air, though Damien tried to fight against it. Damien then involuntarily rose his free hand in front of him. "Jacob please," he begged, "You're better than this!"

"No I'm not." In one swift swing, Jacob beckoned Damien to bring the hammer down on his own hand. A giant crack echoed through the air and a scream of agony emerged from Damien's chest.

"Loki stop," Mr. Boot exclaimed. Jacob ignored him and brought the hammer on Damien's hand again, resulting in another crack and another agonizing blood-curdling scream. Jacob caused Damien to raise the hammer one more time, this time to deliver a fatal blow. Just before he could bring the hammer down on top of Damien's head, a golden spear flew over Fiora and pierced Jacob's leg, impaling him to the sand.

Jacob let out a scream of agony, his influence over Damien's mind immediately disappeared, as did all of his purple fire. Before he passed out from the pain, he looked to where the spear had come from. It was Javi, awakened by

Fiora's screams. "Why Jacob," he said with a lone

tear coming out of his one eye, "Why."

CHAPTER FOURTEEN:

BATTLE HARDENED

Peace had become a stranger to him, though it had only been a few days. Felix, Freyja, and Tyr had fought Draugr around the clock, and they only became more and more bloodthirsty. As much as he hoped they would go away, Felix knew that they wouldn't stop until they were dead or in the clutches of Hel herself. They still had a significant distance between them and the beach, which meant there was still time for a Draugr to attack.

"How far do we have until we get there," Felix asked Freyja.

After a brief moment of silence, Freyja turned to Felix, "Still a long way, five days if we can work with minimal rest." Minimal rest, Felix already felt like he had weights tied to his eyelids. He had not slept well since they arrived on Midgard. They have been walking non-stop the entire time, so much that Felix's feet began to blister and bleed. Rest was the only thing Felix wanted.

"Do you think the Draugr are coming back," he inquired.

Tyr nodded his head, "As long as the sky is dark, absolutely." It was getting hard to tell when the Draugr were coming. When they first arrived, it was easy. Draugr gave off a terrible odor whenever they were nearby. However, the entire world began to smell like them, so it became impossible to know if they were close until it was too late.

Freyja noticed how dismal Felix was

becoming, and while that was appropriate, it wasn't

the way Felix was. "Hey, it's okay. We're going to

get out of this."

Felix chuckled, "You sound so certain."

"Because I am!"

"Freyja, we've already been here too long. I

can feel death inside of me, like my spirit is slowly

fading away." As much as Freyja wanted to be

optimistic, she knew he was right, because she was

feeling the same way.

"We'll find Hel soon Felix, and if not,

perhaps we can rest our souls in the halls of

Valhalla."

Felix furrowed his brow, "We can go to

Valhalla?"

"If Odin permits us, then yes." Felix smiled for a moment, daydreaming about the notion of being able to rest in Asgard's paradise. To the gods, Valhalla was a golden hall with a seemingly infinite number of doors. However, to spirits, it was an entire realm. No god had seen what Valhalla looked like through the eyes of a spirit other than Odin. Felix's smile disappeared as he refocused his attention in front of him, waiting for a Draugr to make itself known.

Freyja didn't know how else to lift his spirits, she was never raised to be that way. She was raised tough and made bitter by the Aesir gods in the Old Age, but times were different now. She was scared that she wouldn't be able to adapt to them. She brushed her long brown hair to the side and recited a poem, a prayer that Njord had taught her when she was just a young god.

Lo there do I see my daughter,

Lo there does she smile at me.

Lo there do I see my son,

Lo there does he call to me.

Lo there do I see my home,

Not in this place, but in their eyes.

Lo there do I see my purpose,

If fate demands it of me, for you I will give my life.

Felix turned towards Freyja, curious about what he just heard. It sounded familiar, as if he had heard it a thousand times before. "What was that," he asked with wonder in his voice.

Freyja smiled, happy that she was able to make her brother less morbid. "That was a poem our father, Njord, made for us."

Felix chuckled, "I didn't know he could be so sentimental."

"He loves us, Felix. That's one thing you won't find in the Aesir. Unconditional, unmoving and never-changing love."

Felix nodded his head, "Is that why we hate them, because they are so hard?"

Freyja smiled for a moment and said, "We don't hate them, Felix. We just set ourselves on a path contrary to theirs. They're battle-hardened, thinking that violence is the only way to solve their problems."

"It's kind of funny," Felix said, "Violence became their downfall eventually."

"It's not really funny to me since you died in that battle, but it is true," Freyja said as her smile disappeared, "That's why we tried to distance ourselves from them."

"Thank you Freyja," Felix said.

"Thank me," Freyja inquired, "Why thank me?"

"For guiding me, for helping me get used to this life. Thank you for teaching me to be a good god."

"Thank you for being a good learner," Freyja said with a smile. If there was ever one thing that made her happy, it was her brother. Whether he was named Felix or Freyr, he seemed the exact same in both lifetimes. He was caring and

fun-loving, but when it was time to remain focused,

he was the most focused god ever. Even though she

had existed for eons, she still looked up to him.

They smiled at each other, happy that they

were able to find some light in this darkness.

Suddenly, Tyr stopped walking and gaped at

the sky. "Hey guys," he said, "Look up." Freyja and

Felix did as he said, and their mouth fell open too.

The dark clouds that were covering the

entire world were suddenly disappearing. As the

were breathing, they realized that their breaths were

less labored. They immediately felt like their

powerful selves again. That could only mean one

thing, Hel was defeated.

"Freyja," Felix said with hope in his voice, "They did it, they stopped her."

Freyja thought about it for a moment. She couldn't believe it, it couldn't possibly be that simple. She stared into the blue sky and searched for something. A feeling, an intuition, something that gave room for doubt. "Felix, I have a bad feeling about this."

"What do you mean, the sky isn't dark anymore. We aren't sick anymore, and neither is anyone else."

Freyja put her hands on Felix's shoulders and faced him towards her. "Brother, in this life we have, not everything that happens is what it appears to be. We are operating outside the will of the fates and are crafting our own Wyrd."

"What the hell does that mean Freyja," Felix asked, slightly annoyed that Freyja couldn't be happy for once.

Freyja took her hands off of Felix and said, "Fate is not at the mortals imagine it brother, it is merely a suggestion of what may be. Though the Norns craft fate, it is not set in stone." She closed her eyes and remembered when she first learned to craft fate herself. The Aesir tried to kill her several times for it, but nonetheless, she never gave up the gift. "We are all able to create the fate we want to have. That is Wyrd, the fate of our own making. However, when we craft fate, it is never as simple as it may seem."

"Freyja, I still have no idea about what that has to do with Hel being defeated."

"I can feel that the battle isn't over brother, it has merely just begun."

Felix shivered at that thought. Sure it was great to be able the breath normally again, but the notion of still having to fight the one responsible for all of what he went through was terrifying. He just wanted to go back to Vanaheim and tend to the crops that he had planted. He wanted to go to Alfheim and learn more elven magic. He wanted to go to any other realm, except for Midgard. He had never wanted to leave Earth so badly.

Freyja saw the fear in his eyes and knelt down to meet him eye to eye. "Felix," she said firmly, "We have come a long way from where we started. We just have to keep moving a little while longer." Her eyes burned with glowing green magic, "Do not let your guard down Felix, this battle is not finished, but it will be soon."

CHAPTER FIFTEEN: A TRAITOR TO THOSE WHO AREN'T MY OWN

Daniel stared out across the ocean, his eyes no longer a burden to him. He could see everything again. He saw what was underneath them, all the life that teamed in the depths of the ocean. He saw the land that lay not so far away, and all the people recovering from a plague that had no cure. However, Daniel also saw that the fight wasn't over. Hel was still there, but she was waiting.

Njord walked up beside Daniel and saw the worry in his eyes, "She's not dead is she?" Daniel shook his head. Njord sighed and bowed his head,

"Well, I do suppose killing the goddess of death is a bad idea anyway."

Daniel looked at Njord confused, "What do you mean, isn't that what we're here to do?"

"Not quite," Njord responded, "As terrible as this all was, Hel is still a very much needed goddess.

"Why," Daniel inquired, "She's way too dangerous to be left on her own!"

"Tell me, Daniel, do your eyes see what happens to the spirits of the dead?"

Daniel furrowed his brow and thought about it. He never was able to see things that weren't living. Seeing the puzzled look on his face, Njord decided to elaborate.

"When we die a death that is unworthy, our spirits go to Helheim. In the old age, Hel took care of the dead there. She made it so that death would still be more enjoyable than life was. However, when she died in Ragnarok, Helheim was thrown into chaos. Spirits escaped and returned to their bodies, taking on the form of Draugr. Your spirits escaped and were reborn into this Mortal world." Njord paused for a moment to let that information sink in. After a few seconds, Njord started again, "As dangerous as she may be, we need Hel to guard Helheim once again."

Daniel nodded his head, but still questioned one thing. "But that would mean if we die, there's no way for us to come back. Our spirits wouldn't be able to escape anymore."

"Precisely," Njord answered, "For what is life without death, without risk of failure. That is what my people, the Vikings lived for. A glorious death."

"I'm sorry, but with all due respect Njord, what's so glorious about dying?"

"Not just dying Daniel, dying with honor."

Suddenly Ryan came up from the bottom deck and hobbled over to his friends. "Guys, he said, "How much longer is it going to take for us to land. I think I'm going to be sick again."

Daniel chuckled lightly at how slurred Ryan sounded. You would think he had drunk all of the mead there was on the ship. "We'll be there in roughly thirty minutes, Njord's boat is moving faster today."

"Okay," Ryan mumbled, "I'm going to go back below deck and feel sorry for myself." Njord and Daniel laughed as Ryan stumbled back down clutching his stomach.

Before long, the beach was visible, and Daniel decided to check on the wellbeing of his friends. However, what he saw dropped his heart to his stomach. "NJORD," he cried to the sea god who was steering the ship, "We have to speed up NOW!"

"Why, what happened?"

"I don't know, but something is wrong!" Indeed, something was terribly wrong. Javi was sitting down in Fiora's arms, and he was so incredibly pale. Jacob was pinned to the ground by Javi's spear, it was straight through his leg.

Damien's hand showed signs of extreme damage, and there was a stranger who was on the beach with all of them.

Njord sped up the boat, using the water to push it forward. He ran it up onto the beach, careful not to hit anyone. As soon as it came to a halt, Njord vaulted over the edge of the longship and ran to Javi and Fiora. Daniel and Ryan went to check on Jacob.

"By the fires of Muspelheim," Njord shouted, "What happened?"

"Hey Njord," Javi groaned, "Good to see you are doing okay."

Fiora smiled, happy that Javi was able to be somewhat optimistic, however, Njord needed to know what the situation was. "We were attacked by

Taliah," she started, "Javi was able to defeat her with magic, but it took all the power he had. He's getting better, but he still needs time."

"Wait," Njord interrupted, "Who is Taliah."

"Someone that I knew from my past," Fiora replied, "It's a long story."

Njord looked behind him and saw Jacob with a spear in his leg. Ryan and Daniel were trying to free him, but a familiar face was instructing them not to. "What's happened to Loki, why is he wounded by Gungnir?"

Fiora shook her head, "He just snapped, Jacob just snapped. He made Damien break his own hand!"

Javi slowly sat up, "Dokkalfar," he whispered, "The Dokkalfar magic he learned, it changed him."

"Oh no," Njord thought. Dokkalfar magic was the strongest magic amongst elven beings. However, the magic was extremely volatile and dangerous to both the target and the user. It could corrupt their thoughts and influence their actions. The practice of the magic was banned in every realm but Svartalfheim. "Why," Njord said, "Why did you let him learn the magic."

Javi shook his head, realizing the error in his ways. "I don't know," he responded, "I thought he was strong enough to resist its darkness."

Njord sighed, this was what he was afraid of. From the moment he met him, Njord knew that

Jacob wouldn't be Jacob for long. His spirit was that of the god of mischief and no matter what, he would be inclined to do what was mischievous. "Javi, you had to have known that letting Loki learn magic that darkens the mind was a terrible idea."

"I know now," Javi said, "Jacob would have never done what he did." He stood to his feet and looked towards his friend, grieved that he had hurt him in the way he did. "You were right Njord," Javi muttered as he looked down towards the sand, "I'm not a good king. I'm not wise enough for this."

Njord put his hand on Javi's shoulder, an action that Javi was not expecting at all. "Javi," he said soothingly, "What I said to you before was said in a fit of anger."

"That doesn't change the fact that I let Jacob get corrupted by Dark Elves. That doesn't change the fact that I made a terrible plan that almost got me and a bunch of other people killed."

"Javi," Njord interrupted, "Being a king does not mean you are perfect, that is an impossible task. You see, being a king is not glamorous as legends would lead you to believe. More often than not, you will find that sometimes, the most uncomfortable seat is the throne."

Javi nodded his head in agreement, because at that moment, Javi didn't want that responsibility. So many lives rested on the decisions that he made. He had just turned 18, he wasn't experienced in this. Sure he did one good thing when he decided not to kill Ymir, but now he was facing the goddess of death. At this point, it was easy for Javi to believe he was not worthy enough to be king of Asgard.

Njord still sensed those doubts and apprehensions, and he couldn't leave him like that. "Javi, in the Old Age, it took eons for me to grow respect for Odin. He was arrogant, impulsive and unnecessarily violent. By the time I honored him, he was already an old god. However, when it comes to you, I see Odin in his latter days, a wise, merciful and kind god. One who if given more time, could have stopped Ragnarok. I sense in you, Javi, a great king."

Javi smiled, eternally grateful that the one who he thought hated him, actually believed in him.

"Thank you Njord," he said, "You are the best of us."

"No, you are." Njord once again look towards Mr. Boot and squinted his eyes, "Do you know who that man is?"

"No, but he helped Damien and Jacob get here, and he tried to help me when Jacob attacked. I trust him."

"And what of my daughter and my son," Njord asked, "Did they make it here with you all."

Javi shook his head, "Then I'm going to go get them myself."

"But that could take forever," Javi replied, "And I don't have the strength to shapeshift."

Njord already knew this to be true, and he had already planned accordingly. "Have Fiora heal Loki, I will use him to find my children."

Javi's eyes widened, "Njord, we can't let him out of our sight, he can't be trusted. Besides, we have time to wait, we stopped Hel."

Njord shook his head, "I'm sorry Javi, Hel is still alive, and she is still is out for our blood."

Javi was taken aback, his knees nearly buckling from the shock. It took everything inside of him to strike her down, but she was still better of than he was. Njord once again put his hand on Javi's shoulder, "It's okay young Odin, it is better this way. We need Hel alive to guard Helheim. We will reconvene here and prepare for battle. Rest and gather your strength, I will go to retrieve my children."

Javi went back to his spot in the sand and told Fiora about Njord's plan, and after a few protests and rebuttals, she agreed to heal Jacob's leg. She walked towards where he was laying and knelt down at his side.

"Fiora," Damien exclaimed, "What are you doing?"

"Njord needs his ability to shapeshift so he can find Freyja and Felix."

"And Javi is okay with this?"

Fiora sighed, "Look, I don't think it's a good idea either, but we have no choice. Taliah... I mean Hel is still coming for us. We need all hands on deck."

With that being said Fiora yanked the spear out of Jacob's leg, resulting in a howl of pain. However, as soon as the spear was free, Fiora used magic to close the wound and ease the pain.

"Loki," exclaimed Njord, "You have become nothing more than a traitor to your family."

"My family," Jacob scoffed, "I didn't betray my family, I lashed out at Damien and gave him what he deserved."

"No Loki," Njord insisted, "You betrayed your people."

"You are *not* my people," Jacob growled, "I am a Jotunn, and I hold no loyalty to either side."

Njord shook his head, "Very well, but nevertheless, you will help me find my daughter, and there will be no tricks. If you refuse, I will kill you. If you betray me I will hunt you down and kill

you, and if you harm my children in any way, there

will be no realm where I will not find you and kill

you. Do you understand?"

Jacob nodded his head, "So intense Njord,

but yes, I understand." Suddenly Jacob's eyes

turned purple as he stared at Njord, trying to take

over his mind. However, Njord's eyes glowed blue

in response. "The mind tricks of the Dokkalfar do

no work on the Vanir. That is your first and final

warning. Your next attempt at trickery will be your

last.

Njord looked at everyone surrounding him

to see who he would take to help keep Jacob in line

during the trip. The one individual stood out of the

bunch, the one they called Mr. Boot. Njord looked into his eyes, he knew who this was, he was a god.

"You," Njord exclaimed, "You come with me."

CHAPTER SIXTEEN: THE GOD OF VENGEANCE

Njord was never really one for flying, he much preferred to be in the sea. However, this was the fastest way to get to his children. With Jacob as a dragon, he could find them within a few hours. Jacob begrudgingly resisted the urge to flip Njord and Mr. Boot off of his back, mainly because Njord promised to decapitate him if he did. Either way, his grudge wasn't really with him, no point in hurting him.

Njord turned back to look at Mr. Boot, debating on whether or not to talk about who he was while Jacob was there. "So, you haven't told them your real name yet. Why?"

Mr. Boot looked up into Njord's blue eyes, "You know very well why, there's no telling who is allied with the sons of Thor, not even you Njord."

The god of the sea chuckled at that ridiculous insinuation, "My allegiance has been, is, and will always be aligned with the Vanir. Either way, you are the strongest god among us, even more so than Magni and Modi."

Mr. Boot shook his head, "It was one mighty deed, lead by rage. I have never been that strong since."

"No my friend, you have only become stronger, you only need to believe it so." Njord looked down towards the ground, "Land here Jacob, they are close." Jacob groaned in his deep dragon voice and started flying down towards the forest that was below.

Once they landed, Njord and Mr. Boot hopped off and Jacob turned back into his normal form. "When I decided to go to Asgard, I did not expect that I would be held prisoner."

Njord almost lashed out on him, but he held his composure, "You should have considered the consequences that came with injuring a god."

"A couple of Idunn Apples and he'll be fine," Jacob shot back.

Njord didn't care about his excuses for what he did. As far as he was concerned, Jacob had proved him to be right. He was, is and will always be the god of mischief. Mr. Boot stuck out his hand and his eyes glowed white. Roots burst through the ground directly underneath Jacob and grabbed him by his ankles.

"Stay here," Mr. Boot commanded, "You cannot be trusted."

"You guys seriously suck," Jacob said through his teeth. His eyes glowed purple as he tried to use magic to escape from the grasp of the roots, but Mr. Boot's magic forbid it. "Man seriously, who the hell are you!"

"You will find out when everyone else does." Mr. Boot and Njord turned and walked deeper into the forest.

Njord looked around fervently, searching for any sign of his children. From what Fiora had told him, Hel was stronger than she was in the Old Age, and she was already insanely powerful.

Mr. Boot saw the anxious look in his eyes, "It is ok Njord, we'll find them soon enough. We will finish our business here and return to Asgard before you know it."

"Will you come with us this time," Njord inquired. None of the other gods had seen Mr. Boot since Ragnarok. Many had believed that he was slain by Magni and Modi.

"I miss home," Mr. Boot replied, "My return is long overdue."

Njord was silent for a moment before speaking again, "Well if you do return, I have a humble request for you."

"And what humble request is that?"

"Javi, your reincarnated father, he has the potential to be the greatest god of us all."

Mr. Boot let a small chuckle escape from his lips, "That means a lot coming from you, given how you felt about my father in the times before."

Njord smiled, knowing this to be true, "He is noble, but he needs guidance. Promise me that you will guide him in the ways of being a king when you all return to Asgard."

"Why don't you," Mr. Boot inquired.

"Because I am no king of Asgard, I am king of Vanaheim, and I am already burdened with teaching my daughter to one day rule over it all."

Mr. Boot thought for a moment, but it wasn't a hard choice. He loved his father, and now he had a chance to reconnect with his spirit again. This was an opportunity that he was not going to let pass him by. "Very well Njord, I will teach him to the best of my ability."

Suddenly, from behind the trees that were in front of them, they heard the voice of his son. "DAD," Felix yelled. Though his feet were killing him, he ran as fast as he could into the arms of his father. Mr. Boot smiled at the embrace and turned his attention towards the woman that was accompanying the boy.

"Freyja," he said with a grin plastered on his face, "It is good to see you again. Time has not altered your beauty."

Freyja looked hard at first, but then realized who she was talking to. "Vidarr," she said joyfully, "I haven't seen you since you killed Fenrir! From the grey in your beard, I can tell you haven't eaten an Idunn Apple in a while."

Vidarr shook his head, "Well, they are hard to come by in this realm." He looked closer at Freyja saw the dirt, grime, and blood that covered her. "You look like you could use an apple too."

Freyja smiled, "The journey has not been kind to us."

"Well, your effort will not be in vain," Vidarr responded, "We will avenge the blood you have shed, and the lives that were lost ."

"And so the rumors are true, Vidarr is the god of vengeance."

"Yes, if that is the god that I need to be."

ᛚᛒᚲᛉᛗᚠᚷᚺᛁᛋᚠᛁᚺᛁᚱᚲᛇᚱᛅᛏᛚᚠᚹᛅᛉ

Taliah had them in view, Njord, Vidarr, Freyja and Freyr, all standing right there with no indication of her presence. It would be so easy now, so easy to slay them where they stood, but she didn't want to risk losing the fight, especially since they all wielded magical abilities.

"Stick to the plan," she said to herself as they began to walk off with each other, "It all will be over soon."

She looked at her hands and saw the dark power crawling underneath her skin. She would never be able to live down the guilt she felt as she thought about what she did to the world. She could never forgive Modi for convincing her to kill so many people.

Still, as she said to herself, it would all be over soon. Before long, every god that came to earth would be gathered on the beach, and there Taliah would summon her army of Draugr. It would overwhelm the gods and their focus would be on stopping them rather than her. She would be able to pick them off one by one.

But then she remembered, Fiora would be there, and she couldn't hurt Fiora. Taliah could never bring herself to cause harm to her sister, even if she wanted to hurt her for what she did. Fiora wouldn't understand or accept what had to be done to the other gods, but Taliah believed she could convince her one day.

The gods had to die so that the world wouldn't face the apocalypse, that had to be true. If it wasn't, then why was she there, why did she have these powers if there was no purpose behind them. She had to do it, she was sure of it.

"I'm the hero of this story," Taliah said as she tried to convince herself, "It's almost over."

CHAPTER SEVENTEEN: THE
END IS NIGH

Javi looked out towards the ocean, watching

the sunrise, knowing it would be the last one before

the battle. Daniel had told him that Taliah was

getting ready to attack. Javi thought about that fact

for a moment, that fact that he knew Hel's earth

name, the fact that she was his girlfriend's adopted

sister. It troubled him because now he was
conflicted.

Taliah was going to fight them with all of
her resolve. In fact, her mission was to kill them,
yet Javi was not allowed to kill her. Njord was right,
they needed a guardian in Helheim. Putting her
there would restore the balance of the living and the
dead. However, Taliah wasn't going to just let that
happen, and Javi knew that this wasn't going wash
as it did with Ymir. Taliah's mind was set and
unchanging. To her, death was the only answer.

Javi gripped his spear and threw it as hard as
he could over the water. It flew incredibly far,
which told him his strength was back. For a moment
he stood there, no spear, no supernatural godly item.
He stood there and did something that he didn't do

much at all before. He stood there as Javi, secure in who he was.

Then he acknowledged the spirit that was inside of him, "I am Odin." He meant that, he felt it. He rooted himself in that present moment, and in doing so, the fears that he had faded away. He knew that he and his companions would find a way to win. He wouldn't fear the future, nor would he fear Taliah. He was Odin, the king of Asgard.

Javi stuck out his hand and recalled the spear. Just as it returned to his hand, he could feel someone walking up behind him.

"Are you holding up okay," Fiora inquired, she had never really seen him act this somber and quiet, except when he was anxious. However Fiora could tell that this wasn't anxious, it was serene.

Javi turned to her and responded, "I'm okay, just getting ready for this fight, mentally at least." Javi took Fiora into his arms and looked her, happy they both made it to the beach together. However, as Javi looked closer into Fiora's green eye, he saw a deep sadness that resided within, "Are you holding up okay?"

Fiora shook her head, "Javi, I know the chance is slim, but if there is any way we can do this without hurting Taliah, please do it."

Javi sighed, wishing he could be more optimistic about the situation, but he wasn't. He was not afraid of the battle, but he knew that the battle could not be avoided. "Fiora, I know you care about her, but I can't promise she won't be hurt. The best-case scenario is that she lives at the end of it, but there will be a fight."

Fiora was fighting to hold back her tears. When their parents were still together, she was Taliah's only friend. She would defend her and fight for her anytime someone would come against her. It broke her heart that now, she would be forced to fight against her. What could have possibly happened that would have turned Taliah into the monster she had become.

"Javi, I know you don't believe me, but the Taliah you know now isn't the one that I know. Something or someone made her do this because she wouldn't on her own."

Javi put his hand around Fiora's waist, hoping that the gesture would be able to soften the blow of his next statement. "Fiora, I'm not here because of who Taliah may have been before, I'm here because of what she did to the world!"

Fiora pulled away from Javi, not because she was mad at him, but because she was trying to find any reason at all to stop the fight from happening. Javi saw the discomfort this was causing her, he completely understood. Just the other night, he was forced to hurt his best friend. As far as he was concerned, people took powers in different ways.

Some people would take their power and use it to defend those without. Some people would use their power for their own personal gain. However, there were some who would use their power to hurt other people. It was a simple concept, but a true one nonetheless. Power in the wrong hands would corrupt user.

"Fiora I'm sorry, but there is going to be a fight. I'll try to make sure she lives, but I'm going to have to fight her." Fiora nodded her head, understanding the situation but still mournful.

Javi continued, "If you want, I could send you to Asgard. You don't have to be here for this if you don't want to."

Fiora's eye snapped towards Javi, who had realized maybe verbalizing this offer was a mistake, "The hell do you mean to go to Asgard? If this fight does happen, I'm your best bet at reasoning with Taliah!"

"You're right, you're right, you're right!" Javi corrected himself, "We need you here, but just know Fiora, if you can't reason with her, I have to do what is best for the nine realms."

"I can reason with her Javi, I know I can." Javi couldn't say with complete honesty that he believed that, so he just nodded his head silently.

Just then, everyone on the beach heard the sound of the flapping of a dragon's wings. Njord had returned with his children. Everyone ran to where Jacob was landing in his dragon form and helped everyone down.

Jacob turned back into his regular form and looked to see who would be the first to try and detain him. His glance turned towards Javi, "I guess you're going to put the spear in my leg again?"

Javi shook his head, "Why man, why did you have to make me do that in the first place."

"I didn't *make* you do anything Javi. You impaled my leg to the ground on your own!"

"And why do you think I did that Jacob," Javi yelled as his eye began to glow golden, "I fought to keep you in Asgard, to show everyone that you weren't like the Loki that lived before, but you have proved me wrong twice Jacob! And to make matters worse, both of those times almost left someone dead!"

Jacob fought for something to say in defense of himself, but he could find nothing, no justifiable excuse for his actions. "You were supposed to be my brother Javi, we look out for each other."

Brothers! Javi was infuriated at this point. Ever since Jacob got his powers, he only used them to amuse himself. From trivial pranks to full-on betrayal, Jacob had never once shown that he had the capacity to use his power for good. Njord was right about him, and Javi knew he couldn't trust Jacob anymore.

"After what you did Jacob, how dare you have the audacity to call me your brother," Javi hissed through his clenched teeth, "I want nothing to do with you, not anymore."

Tears fell from Jacob's glowing purple eyes as his heart broke into a million pieces. Javi commanded Freyja to detain him with her magic, for hers was the strongest out of all of them. Vidarr brought Jacob to the nearest tree and Freyja made the branches wrap around Jacob's entire body. The whole time, Jacob stared at Javi in fury, his eyes glowing brighter and bright er every second.

After it was done, Daniel walked up to Javi and said, "She's coming, Hel… I mean Taliah is coming here now."

Vidarr lowered his head and took a deep breath, "The end is nigh my friends."

"Indeed it is," Javi responded. He turned to everyone else and said, "Prepare for battle, this is the moment we have all been waiting for."

CHAPTER EIGHTEEN: A DANCE WITH DEATH

Ryan sat in the sand, staring down the shoreline of the beach, waiting to see the silhouette of the goddess of death. He wasn't particularly scared of the fight, given that he was invulnerable to pretty much everything. He was even more confident in the outlook of the battle after Freyja conjured up a spell that would lessen the effects of Taliah's death smoke. The only thing that made him nervous was the statement that Njord made in the beginning of their journey.

"No one is invulnerable to death." It echoed in Ryan's mind and reverberated off the walls of his consciousness. Even though his past self was invulnerable as well, he was still killed by a spear of mistletoe. That simple fact proved that even he was vulnerable to death.

Ryan rubbed the rope bindings on his ax, trying his best not to let this nervousness turn into fear. As he stared into the darkness that lay ahead, Tyr came and took a seat right beside him.

"You ready for this," Tyr asked, "I feel like it's going to be completely different from the battle with Ymir."

"What makes you think that," Ryan inquired, even though he felt he already knew the answer.

Tyr ran his fingers across the blade of his sword, "Well for one, we are probably going to fight zombies. For another, we are trying to beat Taliah without killing her."

Ryan chuckled at the thought, though it wasn't really funny at all. The treaty that happened with Ymir was pure luck. Ryan highly doubted that something like that would happen again. As far as he was concerned, there was no way that this fight would end peacefully.

"Well, Javi is the king," Ryan responded, "And even if we think it's stupid, what he says goes."

"What he said almost got Felix killed by Taliah on the first day."

Ryan shook his head, "Death was an obvious risk in the mission, no matter what way we did it."

Tyr sighed, "I guess you're right."

On the other side of the camp, Javi and Fiora sat side by side. Fiora held onto Javi's arm and let her sword lay at her side as she traced the large stone dragon scales on Javi's armor.

"Javi," Fiora started, "Before we fight, please give me a chance to talk to her."

Javi looked down at Fiora and kissed her forehead, "As long as she doesn't attack us right off the bat, you can talk to her."

Fiora smiled dimly, "Thank you, love."

"Hey," Javi said as he felt the uneasiness in her spirit, "Everything will be okay, we'll all get out of this okay."

Fiora shook her head, "That's not what's bothering me. I'm worried more about what happened after."

Javi furrowed his brow, "What do you mean?"

"I don't want Taliah banished to Helheim, I want her in Asgard with us."

Javi sighed, not wanting to be the bearer of bad news, "I'm sorry hon, but we need a guardian of the dead. If Taliah doesn't take her place there, then there is no order."

Fiora shook her head, "No, there's a way that serves everyone, I know it."

"Well I'm always open to suggestions."

Fiora smiled, "I know, that's why you make a great king." She positioned herself to give Javi a kiss on his cheek, but something moved in her spirit that completely derailed her train of thought, and everyone else felt it too.

"Guys," Daniel said dreadfully, "She's here."

He didn't really have to say it, they could all feel it in the cold, bitter air. They could all feel the dread that comes before one takes their last breath, and in a few agonizing seconds, they saw her. A dark silhouette was standing in the distance staring at all of the gods, some of whom were trembling in fear.

There was a moment of silence between the gods, neither of them knowing what they would say to each other, neither one knowing what to do. Suddenly, the silence broke as Fiora charged forward to get a closer look at Taliah.

"Hey sis," she cried out, "Is that you."

Taliah didn't say anything at first, but after a few moments, she spoke, "Now you want to call me a sister!"

"I'm sorry Taliah," Fiora shouted, "I was mad before, I didn't mean it!"

Taliah fought back the tears that were pushing against her eyelids. She was not looking forward to this moment. She would try to convince Fiora that she needed to let her do this, but it wouldn't work. Fiora would try to be a hero just like her mom and try to persuade her against it. It wouldn't work, and they would fight, and Taliah could only hope that Fiora would be standing at the end of it.

"You won't understand why I have to do this," Taliah shouted, "I'm sorry but you can't change my mind."

Fiora shook her head, "You're right Taliah, I don't understand why you want to kill us, but whatever reason you have, I know it's wrong."

"He told me you would say that!"

Fiora was taken aback by that statement, but she was relieved. The fact that someone else was involved meant that killing everyone wasn't fully her idea. "Who told you that?"

Taliah opened her mouth to say it, but something held her back, "You can join me sister, we can both save the world and become the rulers of Asgard. Just me and you, just like before."

"Taliah," Fiora pleaded, "Mom wouldn't want you to do this!"

"Well mom isn't here is she!" Taliah refused to succumb to that guilt, "Our mommy left me with that monster that she hid you from."

"Taliah, that wasn't her choice."

The goddess of death shook her head. It was time to stop talking, this was only going to happen one way, "We all have a choice sister. She made hers, and I made mine."

Taliah rose her hands to the sky as her eyes turned pitch black. Dark smoke surrounded her hands and traveled down her arms. Damien threw

Mjolnir at her midsection, but the hammer passed

right through her. "Oh crap," Damien responded.

"Taliah, please," Fiora said as she tried to

reach her sisters heart one last time, "Don't do this."

"I love you Fiora," without waisting another

second, Taliah brought her hands down into the

sand, sending the power of death under the ground.

It started to shake violently and Javi started to think

that she had just summoned a giant to step on all of

them, but then the sand started moving. It looked

like something was trying to climb up.

In the distance, still bound to the tree, Jacob

yelled, "I think I'd like to go back to Asgard now!"

At that moment, so did everyone else,

especially when the first rotten hand burst through

the sand just a few feet from them. The hand pulled the rest of its body upon the ground, and in a few seconds, a Draugr stood, contorted and broken.

Javi hoped that the Draugr would be the only foe they would have to face. He hoped that the shaking in the ground didn't mean anything, but he knew it did. In the short few seconds following, hundreds of hands burst through the ground and the hundreds of Draugr that the hands belonged to lifted themselves out of the ground.

At first, they were all confused, looking at their broken and dislocated bones snap back into place. They mumbled and murmured to each other, wondering what had just interrupted their eternity.

Taliah looked at her living dead army and said, "Mortal souls, I am sorry I have left you behind. It hurts me to know that you have been left to the cold dark winds of Helheim, but I'm back now, and I will never leave you again."

For the last time, Taliah looked at Fiora's pleading eyes. She knew that this moment was it, and what she did next would literally determine the future of the universe. For a moment, she felt like maybe the responsibility would be better if it was on someone else's shoulders. However, Taliah knew that someone worse than her would do it anyway.

She looked back towards the Draugr and said, "Kill the gods that stand before you, and you will have a home with me in the kingdom of Asgard!" The Draugr gasped at the thought. Their souls were damned to Helheim from the moment they left their bodies, and without Hel there to care for them, Helheim was cold, dark and uncared for. Every soul suffered and yearned for a better eternal home. This was their chance.

At first, none of them moved, as they were waiting for someone to go first. It seemed like an eternity that they were standing there, staring at the kings and queens of the higher realms. But suddenly one brave Draugr shouted a war cry and charged forward.

That was all they needed, just one of them to charge forward at the gods, that was their cue. With that one brave Draugr leading the horde, the rest of them swarmed towards the gods like a sea of rotten flesh. Javi gripped his spear tightly in his hands and charged back at them, followed by the rest of the gods. Within seconds the living and the dead were upon each other and the battle began.

Javi's one eye glowed as he immersed himself in the spirit of battle. Draugr flocked towards him on all sides as he swung his spear around cutting off the heads of as many Draugr as he could. That was the only way to kill them, they had to lose their head.

As Javi dodged the attacks from the hundreds of Draugr swarming him, he failed to see the one that knew what the abilities of the Draugr were. A risen Norseman rose closed his eyes and summoned the magic of the Draugr, and in seconds he had grown to the size of a Jotunn.

Javi realized this far too late and tried his best recover. He cut at the Draugr's knees, but it didn't phase it at all. The monster grabbed Javi and threw him across the battlefield, straight towards Taliah. Though it seemed as if she was right in his path and would break his fall, he passed right through her body, leaving her unharmed and giving Javi a rough landing. He bounced and skidded across the sand, leaving him bruised and cut in many areas as the goddess of death walked up to him.

"Taliah," he said, trying not to sound like he was begging, "Whoever told you that you had to do this, they are lying to you."

"And what makes you so much more trustworthy," Taliah snapped back, "He told me everything. The world ended before because of you, I can't let that happen again."

She lunged towards Javi, firing black smoke at him relentlessly. Javi recovered quickly and jumped out of the way again and again and again, expertly dodging Taliah's attacks. "STAY STILL," she cried, not wanting this fight to draw out longer than it had to.

"Taliah, you aren't thinking straight," Javi shouted. He threw his Gungnir at her and immediately realized his mistake. The spear passed right through her, and at the last second before it was out of her grasp, she grabbed it and swung it back towards Javi.

Taliah was a lot stronger than he thought she was, and Javi had to constantly bob and weave in order to not get struck down by his own weapon. However, as Javi was dodging the spear, he realized something. Taliah didn't know how to fight with the spear. She was swinging it sloppily and predictably.

Javi timed her attacks and caught his weapon, gripping the shaft right below the spearhead. As fast as he could, Javi summoned the spirit of battle and put all of the power from inside of him inside of Gungnir. In one fantastic golden explosion, magic burst from the spear and sent both of them flying apart from each other.

Both of them were rendered unconscious for a moment, but Taliah was getting back up in a few seconds. As she was inching her way towards him, Javi looked up and saw the battle ensuing in the distance. His friends were managing, but he feared they couldn't hold on for too much longer. This dance with death had to end.

CHAPTER NINETEEN: LO THERE DO THEY CALL

Damien's hand was killing him, but he knew he had to get his act together if he was going to win this fight. Almost everyone was trying to make sure the dead didn't tear them to pieces, but almost no one was trying to take on the giant one, and he was causing the most issues.

"Alright," he said, "I'll do it myself. He rose Mjolnir to the sky and summoned an enormous bolt of lightning to surround him. Every tingly shock from the bolt charged his adrenaline and gave him energy. He ran as fast he could towards the giant Draugr, electrifying everything that was in his way.

Damien remembered all of the great feats he took part in. He killed a Jotunn by himself with a single stroke of his hammer, he fought a dragon in Svartalfheim, and now he was fighting an army of the dead. He was powerful, no matter how broken his hand was, he was powerful.

He jumped into the air and launched himself towards the Draugr's head. It saw him, but Damien was moving much too quickly for him to be struck by it. He reeled back his hammer, and as soon as he was close enough, Damien swung the hammer into the Draugr's temple with the force of the strongest lightning bolt. A blinding flash and a deafening boom silenced the rest of the Draugr as they saw the giant completely disintegrate from the force of the hit. Damien landed on the ground, and every single Draugr had their eyes on him.

Njord saw it, and he knew that no matter how powerful Damien was, the full force of Hel's Draugr army would overwhelm him. As all of the Draugr ran to swarm Damien, Njord turned to the other gods and yelled, "DEFEND THOR!" all of the gods chased after the Draugr to stop them from hurting Damien. Upon seeing this, Njord turned and saw Javi fighting the goddess of death by himself. At that moment, he realized he had to help him, Javi would not win on his own. He turned back towards the fight with the Draugr and saw his children valiantly cutting down the army of the dead. He took a deep breath and recited the poem he had sung

for them oh so often.

> *Lo there do I see my daughter,*
>
> *Lo there does she smile at me.*
>
> *Lo there do I see my son,*
>
> *Lo there does he call to me.*
>
> *Lo there do I see my home,*
>
> *Not in this place, but in their eyes.*
>
> *Lo there do I see my purpose,*
>
> *If fate demands it of me, for you I will give my life.*

He didn't know why he felt compelled to do

that, but he felt better now that he did. He turned

back towards Javi and ran to aid him. His eyes

began to glow blue as he summoned whatever

magical power he had. Taliah's back was facing

him as she was firing that deathly smoke at Javi.

Njord charged his sword with his magical strength and sliced at Taliah's backside. The pure magic that laced the blade sliced through her skin. It wasn't deep, but Taliah felt it. She turned and shot a blast of death at Njord, blowing him back several feet. He recovered quickly, but the smoke definitely weakened him.

With her attention fully focused on Njord, Javi copied what he saw him do. He sent his power into his spear until it was glowing red-golden, but instead of sending out a golden blast, he kept it inside and jabbed the spear towards Taliah's leg. He meant to completely impale her leg, but his vison was impaired by his weakened state. Either way, Taliah was hurt by it and one hit after another, she was starting to get beaten to the ground.

Taliah was infuriated, and the pain from the magical cuts burned like fire. An unholy and dark rage grew inside of her, an instinct lead not by her mind, but by the spirit inside of her. Her eyes once again turned pitch black, sucking the light out of the surrounding area. The dark side of her face was covered in dark runes, and dark smoke poured uncontrollably out of her skin.

She opened her mouth and screamed an ear-splitting scream that was heard all across the beach. A dark explosion that came from Taliah blew Njord and Javi away, sending them skidding across the ground. They landed beside each other, still somehow holding on to their weapons.

"Javi," Njord said, "We have almost won this fight. If we defeat Hel, then the Draugr will follow, they only stand because of her power."

"I don't know if I can, I don't have that much more power in me."

Njord jumped to his feet and helped Javi to his, "Then fight to the death, for the glory of Asgard." Those words struck Javi's spirit because it reminded him of the time when he knelt beside Fiora after her journey to Mimir's well. It reminded him of the message that she had taught him. He wasn't there so that he could live, he was there so that others could. That was the burden of a king.

As Taliah stood up while her wounds were quickly healing, Javi ignored the pain that came from his own. He was focused entirely on Taliah and charged his spear with the last remaining magic he had within him. "For the glory of Asgard."

Njord and Javi charged at Taliah and started swinging their weapons at her. However, their confidence in their victory diminished when Taliah's skill in fighting back drastically improved. It was like she knew what they were going to do before they did. She dodged and counterattacked with expertise, almost as if she were programmed to do it. The goddess of death inside of her took full control.

Javi swung his spear as skilled as he could, but she dodged every single stroke and swatted his away like a fly. Without Javi in the way, Taliah was able to focus completely on Njord and he began to feel as if she was overpowering him. He blocked her swings and tried to attack her back, but it was becoming increasingly difficult.

Javi saw Njord's struggle and knew he had to do something. If he didn't he knew Njord wasn't going to live. As much as he didn't want to, he saw no other way. Taliah had to die in order for the battle to end because she wasn't going to willingly stop. While she was completely focused on Njord, Taliah's back was completely unguarded. One clean jab with his spear would finish her.

Javi stood to his feet and lunged towards Taliah with his spear in position to strike her down once and for all. This was what had to happen, that's what he kept telling himself. He knew someone had to guard Helheim, and it would probably be him to volunteer, but Taliah needed to die.

He thrust his spear as hard as he could, aiming straight towards where her heart would be. Javi had only realized his mistake when he saw that his spear lacked a certain glow.

He had forgotten to charge the spear with magic, which meant that it was going to cause Taliah no harm. Gungnir passed straight through Taliah and went straight into Njord's chest.

"NOOO," Javi cried from the top of his lungs. He ran as fast as he could to catch Njord before he hit the ground. As he knelt by his side, Javi panicked, trying to best figure out how to fix him. He was alive, but he was slipping away.

"I'm so sorry Njord," he sobbed, "I'm so sorry." Javi was so in despair, he didn't realize that Taliah was walking up behind him raising her hand to deliver a fatal blow, but something was moved in her.

As she saw Javi mourning over his fallen comrade, she realized something. Modi had described the gods as ruthless animals. That they had no regard for life and that Ragnarok happened because they did it on purpose. She was told they were monsters, but what she was looking at wasn't a monster. She saw a person, a legitimately good person.

At this point, she knew she wasn't the hero of this story, she was the villain. She had needlessly caused so much pain and suffering, and now she was leading a battle to kill those that tried to stop it. Taliah finally knew that she was wrong, this was not her destiny.

She couldn't fix everything, but she knew she could stop this battle. Taliah rose her hand to the Draugr army and sucked her power away. Immediately, their souls were sent back to Helheim. Their decomposed bodies sunk back into the ground.

Confused at first, the rest of the gods turned towards where Javi and Njord were fighting the goddess of death. Their jaws dropped open when they saw Taliah comforting Javi, who was holding the god of the sea in his arms. Freyja screamed when she saw Javi's golden spear sticking out of his chest.

Felix and Freyja ran towards them, followed by the rest of the gods. "FATHER," Freyja cried as she and Felix slid on the ground towards Njord's side.

"My children," Njord whispered, "Are... are you okay."

"Don't worry about us," Felix said as he was trying to hold back the tears pushing against his eyelids, "Can you heal him Freyja!?"

"I'm going to try!" Freyja slowly pulled the spear from Njord's chest, and pushed her hand against the wound, resulting in many pained groans from Njord. Her eyes began to glow green as she summoned every healing ability she had. However, as soon as the healing power began to flow into his, Njord rose his hand and grabbed his daughter's wrist.

"No," he said quietly, "Please, no."

Freyja's eyes turned back to their normal auburn-green color, tears began to fall across her face, "Father, what do you mean no? I can fix you, I can save you!"

"My daughter," Njord paused and coughed up small drops of blood, "I have been alive far longer than even I can comprehend. It is my time to join those who came before me."

"Dad please," Felix begged, "You aren't thinking straight. You don't have to die!"

"But what is life's meaning without death my son," he coughed up more blood, Njord could feel his soul slipping away. He raised his hand and touched Freyja's cheek, "Lo there do I see my daughter, lo there does she call to me."

He turned and touched Felix's cheek, "Lo there do I see my son, lo there does he call to me." He looked at both of his children, "Lo there do I see my home, not in this place but in their eyes."

Njord coughed violently one last time, "Lo there do I... see my purpose, for you... for you..."

Njord's gaze turned towards the sky, "Oh wow, this is...what it's like." After a few more tired and labored breaths, Njord's chest fell one more time as his final breath escaped past his lips.

CHAPTER TWENTY:

FALLEN TEARS AND A

BURNING SHIP

After Njord passed on Midgard, the courts of Vanaheim were flooded with sorrow. Many found the manner in which he died suspicious, especially since he was killed by Javi's spear. Felix took it the worst, and ever since then, he didn't utter a word.

However, today would be Njord's funeral, and every creature in Asgard and Vanaheim would be there. Even Ymir and a select few of the Jotnar were going to attend. Fiora tried to see if Taliah

would go, but Taliah opted to go to Helheim and

see if she could fix what her absence had caused.

Either way, it was to be an honorable event, and

Javi fully intended to be there

He had just finished putting on the golden

armor that Brokkr had repaired for him. He looked

at himself in the silver mirror by the door of his

room. Of course, he looked sharp and godly, and his

scars from the battle were healing fine, but Javi

didn't see himself as a hero. If it weren't for him,

Njord would still be alive. He could never forgive

himself for that.

"You know, it was his choice to go," Fiora

had just walked into Javi's room and sat on his bed,

"I think it was his fate."

Javi walked away from the mirror and took a seat beside her, "Me and you both know that fate can change based on our actions. He didn't have to die."

"But he wanted to, Javi..."

"Fiora, please," Javi interrupted, "There's nothing anyone can say that can change my mind."

Fiora sighed, knowing that he was being honest. "Well, it's time for us to go. They're going to be burning the boat in a few hours."

Javi nodded his head and stood, "Then let's get to Vanaheim."

Javi and Fiora gathered everyone that resided in the court of Asgard (Except for Jacob, who they had imprisoned after returning to Asgard) and went to the realm travel room. In silence, they all stepped through the portal that led to Vanaheim

and made their way to the castle.

It was as if the realm itself was mourning for

the loss of their king. The rain was pouring from the

sky and lightning danced in the clouds. The only

shelter from the weather where the castle grounds.

Once they stepped into the castle's throne room,

they saw the large gathering of creatures inside that

came to pay their respects the fallen god.

Vanaheim's throne room was drastically

different from Asgard's. For one, there were only

three thrones, and they were made out of polished

wood. For another, The entire back of the castle was

exposed to the outdoors, and it faced the oceans of

Vanaheim. A large black longship was sitting on the

water.

"Javi," a voice shouted from behind. It was Freyja, she was wearing a long black dress with a hood covering her head. "Thank you for coming," she said, "It really means a lot to us."

Javi forced a smile, "Njord taught me everything I needed to know about being a god. If would have been wrong for me not to."

Freyja wiped a tear from her eye, "Even after the battle of Jotunheim, he spoke kindly of you. He may not have approved of every decision you made, but he knew you would be a good god, at least better than how Odin was before."

Javi had a hard time believing that, After that battle, he and Njord were not on good terms. But Freyja had no reason to lie, so it must have been true. If that were the case Njord was much more honorable than he thought.

"Thank you, Freyja," Javi responded, "How's Felix doing?"

Freyja lowered her head, "Not as good as I hoped he would. I've had thousands of years with my father, Felix barely had one. He's still angry, but I'm sure he'll come along."

"Freyja, I can't even begin to explain how sorry I am."

"Don't be, It is the cost that comes with battle. Not everyone will live, but he died at peace because he died honorably."

Freyja turned toward the back of the throne room, towards the waters that lied beyond. "It is time to say goodbye." Freyja walked to the thrones and stood in front of the one that was in the center.

"Creatures of all realms," she began, "It is an honor that you have chosen to spend this moment with us! My father, Njord, always felt alone in this realm, that he had no friends beyond, but your gathering here today warms his spirit. As we honor his legacy today, let us remember how he shaped the Nine Realms in the time he spent with us, how he helped us rebuild after Ragnarok, and how he protected us against the treacherous acts of Magni and Modi."

Freyja looked towards Javi and the other Aesir gods, "Let us remember how he took time to raise the next generation!" She grabbed the sword that laid on the throne behind her. It was her father's, but now the legacy was passed on. Freyja

was now the queen of Vanaheim and it's sole ruler.

She would make her father proud. She rose the

sword and shouted "TO NJORD, THE GOD OF

THE SEA!"

Every creature in the room, Jotnar,

Dwarven, Elven, Valkyrie and godly rose their

weapons and shouted, "TO NJORD, GOD OF THE

SEA!" The statement was followed by ear-splitting

shouts and the sound of swords clanging together as

the mass of creatures followed Freyja down to the

beach. Before long the were standing in front of the

massive longship. Freyja and Felix climbed aboard

to say their goodbyes to their father.

They walked to the middle of the ship that

where the pyre was set up, Njord's body was lying

on top of it. "Father," Freyja began, "I will not disappoint you."

She grabbed Njord's trident from the ground beside the pyre. Njord had not used the trident since the battle of Ragnarok, It became more like scepter than a weapon. However, it was always a prize to him and it was priceless to Freyja. She did not feel worthy enough to wield it, so she deemed it necessary to lay it to rest with Njord. Freyja placed the trident on Njord's body and backed away from the pyre.

Felix stepped forward and said, "Goodbye dad, I will find justice for what was done to you." Freyja looked at her brother concerned. She would really have to focus on cooling the anger that resided within him. Felix placed his hand on Njord's head and stepped away from the pyre.

Freyja put her hand on Felix's back and said, "It's time to go, brother, I'll meet you on the beach." Felix nodded his head and quickly walked towards the back of the boat and jumped back onto the beach. Freyja took one last look at her father's body and whispered, "I love you."

Without waiting another moment, Freyja lowered the sails on the ship and jumped off of the back onto the beach. The ship was sailing away from the shore incredibly fast and Freyja wished she could make it go slower. She already saw the archer Valkyrie raising their burning arrows towards the boat. Freyja knew that this was her father's last voyage, and she knew that in a few minutes, she would see the boat become engulfed in flames.

"Far vel, faðir," Freyja whispered as the flaming arrows streaked across the sky. In her native tongue, that meant, "Goodbye, father." It felt more personal, more real, and tears streamed down her face as the arrows landed on the boat and the flames began to spread. In a few seconds, the boat was entirely aflame. All of the creatures that stood on the beach waited until the ship disappeared past the horizon.

CHAPTER TWENTY-ONE:

FOOL ME ONCE, FOOL ME

TWICE

Javi sat on his throne looking at all of his

comrades sitting in their respective thrones as well.

One thing resonated in his mind as he anticipated

the events that were about to unfold, the throne truly

was the most uncomfortable seat. In a few seconds,

two Valkyrie would walk through the entrance of

the throne room, holding Jacob within their grasp.

Javi would have to inform Jacob of his fate, decided

by the court of the Aesir.

"BOOM," the giant doors opened and the two Valkyrie walked into the throne room. Between them was Jacob, his hands and feet were chained with heavy iron. It pained Javi to see his friend like this, but he knew it had to be done. Jacob wasn't on their side anymore.

"Hello Javi," he said sarcastically, "It's a pleasure to see you again. That dungeon definitely isn't as nice as the castle."

"Don't try to guilt-trip me, Jacob," Javi snapped back, "You knew the consequences that came with hurting one of our own."

"Look, man, I get it, I messed up, but you have to believe me I won't do it again." He sounded sincere, but Javi knew better. No matter what he would always be the god of mischief, he would

always harbor that spirit.

"You fooled me once on Jotunheim, and you

fooled me twice on Midgard. I will not let you fool

me again."

Jacob let tears fall down his face, in hopes it

would show Javi that he was sincere, that he

wouldn't let the Dokkalfar magic corrupt his

thinking again. "Just give me another chance Javi! I

promise I'll do anything to earn your trust again."

Javi shook his head, "I'm sorry Jacob, but

the decision had been made." Javi looked at Tyr. As

the god of justice, Tyr saw it fit for him to deliver

the sentence that they had decided upon.

Tyr stood to his feet and said, "Jacob, due to

the nature and severity of your crimes, you are

banished from Asgard for all of eternity, effective immediately. Your actions have proven that you are not worthy of a throne."

"Javi," Jacob shouted as he lept towards him, held back by the Valkyrie, "Please don't let them do this to me! I'm your friend, your brother!"

Javi was silent for a moment, but then he made direct eye to eye contact with Jacob and said, "You *were* my brother Jacob, I don't know who you are anymore." With those final words, Javi motioned towards the Valkyrie, and they began to take him way from the throne room and to the realm travel room where he would be thrown into the Midgard portal.

Silent tears fell from Javi's eyes as he saw his friend kicking and screaming as he was being dragged out of the throne room. If all went well,

Javi would never see his old friend again, and that

broke his heart more than anything else ever did.

ᛁᛒᚲᛊᛗᚠᚷᚺᛁᛊᚠᚦᚺᛁᛈᚲᚼᚱᚼᛏᚾᚠᛈᚢᚼᛁ

As Modi stood in the open field, he could

sense that while these events didn't transpire as he

thought they would, it all still worked out the same

way. Hel was in Helheim, which meant the souls of

fallen gods wouldn't return.

There was also a rift within the courts of

Asgard. Loki had been cast out, which meant there

was room for anger and revenge in his heart. It was

that same anger and revenge that motivated him to

lead Ragnarok in the old age. If this anger could be

controlled, Modi knew he could use Loki to bring

destruction to the reborn gods.

Magni walked behind his brother Modi, his veins pulsating in his arms. "It is our time now brother," he said, "We should strike Asgard now."

Modi chuckled at his brother's haste, "After all these years, you still bear no sense of occasion."

"What or who in any of the realms do we have to wait for now," Magni demanded to know.

"Loki," Modi responded, "He has just been banished from Asgard." Magni's blue eyes widened, but then they quickly went back to a sneer.

"And why should that mean anything to me? We don't need a slippery little prankster to get rid of the gods."

Modi nodded, "No we don't, but I don't want Loki to be the one to get rid of them. I want him to be the one that tears them apart, from the inside. We will destroy what is left."

To Be Continued In:

Rulers of Asgard

A Trick of Light

Made in the USA
San Bernardino, CA
19 March 2020

65833755R00180